AFTER FROST

AFTER FROST

An Anthology of Poetry from New England

Edited with an introduction and commentary by

Henry Lyman

UNIVERSITY OF MASSACHUSETTS PRESS
Amherst

Published in association with
THE NEW ENGLAND FOUNDATION FOR THE HUMANITIES
Boston

Copyright © 1995 by
New England Foundation for the Humanities

University of Massachusetts Press edition, 1996

All rights reserved
Printed in the United States of America
LC 96-20905
ISBN 1-55849-041-8

Library of Congress Cataloging-in-Publication Data

> After Frost : an anthology of poetry from New England / edited with an
> introduction and commentary by Henry Lyman.
> > p.   cm.
> > Rev. ed. of a work first produced in a limited ed. by the New England
> Foundation for the Humanities.
> > Includes bibliographical references. (p.   ).
> > ISBN 1-55849-041-8 (pbk. : alk. paper)
> > 1. American poetry —New England. 2. Frost, Robert, 1874–1963—
> Influence. 3. American poetry—20th century. 4. New England—Poetry. I.
> Lyman, Henry, 1942–   .
> > PS541.A5   1996
> > 811' .5080974—dc20   96-20905
> >   CIP

This volume was originally created by the New England Foundation for the
Humanities as the text for its "After Frost" project. With support from the
New England humanities councils and funding from the National
Endowment for the Humanities, the "After Frost" reading and discussion
series was presented at more than thirty libraries throughout New England.

The New England Foundation for the Humanities promotes understanding
of the humanities through programs in libraries, museums, and from these
state humanities organizations:

> Connecticut Humanities Council
> Maine Humanities Council
> Massachusetts Foundation for the Humanities
> New Hampshire Humanities Council
> Rhode Island Committees for the Humanities
> Vermont Council on the Humanities

Acknowledgments for permission to reprint material under copyright begin
on page 239.

Table of Contents

—

II. My Own Desert Places

AFTER FROST

Introduction

⁓

This book was originally produced in a limited edition by the New England Foundation for the Humanities, for use in a series of public discussions offered in New England libraries. Five hundred copies migrated through the six states, from library to library, and returned in the end contentedly thumbworn. This larger, slightly revised edition still has the same aims. One of these is simply to reaquaint readers with the poet most widely identified with the region and render for consideration, and pleasure, related poems by thirty New Englanders who follow him in time. Another is to show that there is life after Frost: that New England poetry grows and moves, and continues to move us. Still another is to provide an occasion for looking into matters of importance to us all, by way of poems occurring for the most part in New England landscapes, townscapes, and cities.

After an introduction touching on Frost, his language, and the subjects of his and the other poems in the book, there are four sections of poetry, each introduced by a page or two of prose. Every section has the same sequence of poets, one poem from each, their poems converging on a common field of view. The poets, drawn from the six New England states, appear chronologically by birth date, each section beginning with Frost and moving through the century to Martín Espada. Not all the poets are native, not even Frost himself, who was born in San Francisco in 1874 and lived there until the age of eleven. Nor should they be seen as the only, or "best," poets of New England. They are a few among many, past and present, acclaimed or not, who happen to have spent much of their lives here and written poems having to do with New England places. So this anthology is by no means comprehensive; nor is it in any sense a canon. Rather it is simply a selection of poems chosen for clarity and depth and common ground. While speaking with very different voices, the poems tend to converse with one another from page to page, and I trust you will hear more consonance than pandemonium.

Though I used the word "subjects" a moment ago, I doubt that any of these poems was begun with a definite subject in mind, or if so it probably changed as the poem evolved. "A poem," Frost wrote to a friend in 1915, "positively must not begin thought first. It finds the thought and the thought finds the words." A poem, that is, whether it begins with the vaguest notion, a feeling, a mental image, a phrase, or a combination of these, usually discovers what it is thinking about only as it is being written. I hope that the readers of this book will arrive at a poem's "subject" in a similar way: by letting it come to them as they read, enjoying first of all the poem's events—its sounds and images, and the magic made when language seems to become what it describes. Gradually a picture should develop, itself a window through which to view what the poem has come to ponder, whether it be nature, the individual, a society, or whatever.

Buttering Parsnips

The rumpled white-haired figure of the aging Robert Frost still towers over the century, and the character he projected of a salty, benevolent, wittily cantankerous Yankee is so ingrained in memory that if you stopped someone on the street today and asked them to name a poet it would probably be him. His poems are still revered in classrooms across the country, and no other American poet, not even Longfellow in the last century, was as highly celebrated. Four Pulitzers, honorary degrees, the Academy of American Poets Fellowship, the Bollingen Prize, and two Congressional citations—not to mention public readings attended by thousands, his reading at a presidential inauguration, and his private meeting with a Soviet premier—made him headline news for a while, and the fact that the press could have given more space to a poet than the latest ballgame seems almost blasphemous. With the impulse to idolize, however, came sentimentalization, and his poems were read more often for a nostalgic moral uplift than a realistic view of living. Eventually Frost himself began to play the role of the rustic farmer-philosopher-poet we wanted him to be, allowing us to maintain an illusion that poets are kindly, simple, earthy, and essentially harmless. But when the three-volume Thompson biography began emerging a few years after Frost's death, people were shocked to learn that he had a darker side. The figure that emerges there is relentlessly ambitious, self-defensive, and vindictive. Moreover it is implied that the tragedies that beset his family—among them the mental illness of a daughter and the suicide of a son—because he blamed himself, were Frost's responsibility. Thompson's portrait is biased, but it led many who had been taken in by the public, pastoral Frost to feel they had been duped, and some reversed their positions accordingly. This turnabout may have strengthened the equally debilitating myth that poets are hopeless neurotics who have little to do with the rest of us.

Frost was neither mask nor monster, but humanly complex and contradictory. Though his children were overshadowed by him, he filled their childhood with story-telling and adventure, as well as companionship, and struggled to help them in their troubled adult lives. Ambitious and competitive he was; but he was also generous in his way, a gifted teacher, accessible and outgoing, as willing to encourage the young and aspiring as he was to disparage his peers. And there were causes, as well as reasons, for his combativeness.

His boyhood in San Francisco was clouded by his parents' financial woes, and the combination of a bullying alcoholic father and an indulgent spiritually minded mother contributed to an emotional instability deepened by his father's death, the uprooting of Frost and his younger sister, and the resettlement of the family with in-laws in Lawrence, Massachusetts. A spotty education, the long and frustrating courtship of his high school classmate Elinor White, their contentious early years of marriage, and the death of their first child, Elliott, doubtlessly intensified his sense of insecurity and the need to prove himself. He wanted to lead the life of a poet-farmer, independent from the mainstream. Other children came quickly, however, and his seven-year attempt at subsistence farming in New Hampshire taught him the hardship of providing for a family of six while trying to preserve time and mind for poetry. His brief matriculations at Dartmouth and Harvard allowed him to teach school at least, but more than a decade of writing without book publication must have taken a toll on his self-esteem. Even after the turning-point, when, at the flip of a coin, he and Elinor took the family to London, where he shortly found a publisher for his first book and not long afterwards his second, it seems that he could never quite trust his luck. Or, to put it differently, by the time an American edition of the latter made the best-seller list he seemed to have trusted his luck sufficiently to make the most of it when it came his way.

This he did, sometimes with a certain playfulness, often by manipulating and finagling. Because we want our poets to be as pure as their poetry, his behavior was considered distasteful and worse, by Thompson and others. Yet Frost had learned from experience that the literary marketplace is as competitive as any other, and there was *real* competition, in academic circles, from the more cerebral poetry of T.S. Eliot and Ezra Pound. Besides, he was in need of money, for himself and (until her death in 1938) Elinor, and also for their children, who were a constant source of worry well beyond his middle age. Royalties and reading tours helped, and teaching appointments at colleges and universities provided relative security, yet it was not until his seventy-fourth year that he received permanent light-duty employment, at

Amherst College, with the promise of a pension. But even with his future insured, and his *Collected Poems* published, Pulitzered, and selling in record numbers, it seemed he could never receive enough prestige. He was made a roving cultural ambassador, collected honorary degrees from Oxford and Cambridge, read at Kennedy's inauguration, and, just a few months before his death in 1963, traveled to the Soviet Union and had his rather poignant meeting with Khrushchev. Sadly, in those remaining years, his habit of playing the Yankee poet became a sort of caricature, more pitiable, perhaps, than offensive.

Yet by hook or crook, and mostly by dint of his poems, he had succeeded in what he set out to do. He stated his objectives clearly in a letter written from London in 1913, two years before his second book, *North of Boston,* was published in New York: ". . . there is a kind of success called 'of esteem' and it butters no parsnips. It means a success with the critical few who are supposed to know. But really to arrive where I can stand on my legs as a poet and nothing else I must get outside that circle to the general reader who buys books in their thousands. I may not be able to do that. I believe in doing it—don't doubt me here. I want to be a poet for all sorts and kinds." That he is, and is still read by them. Had he not sought popularity, his poetry might not have moved beyond a "critical few" to you and me. It stands to his credit that he was able to put it in our hands.

Our Ancient Speech

The urge to speak to "all sorts and kinds" echoes thoughts of Emerson, whom Frost always admired, and whose poetry his mother had read to him in childhood. Every human being is a poet, Emerson believed, in the sense that each of us has the capacity to feel profound wonder in the presence of natural objects: ". . . every man is so far a poet as to be susceptible of these enchantments of nature; for all men have the thoughts whereof the universe is a celebration." But wonder asks for expression, and without expression "man is only half himself." The other half had been drowned out, as it were, by the noise of commerce: not by horsedrawn wagons and the hubbub of the marketplace, but by dull, decadent, overused words—the rootless, abstract language or "paper currency" of an alienated urban society. True expression, the solid picture-language of poetry, was to cut through such noise, reunite us with nature and ourselves, and speak to the poet in everyone.

Frost wanted his own poetry to have a similar effect. Addressing the reader in the poem "Directive" (the last in this book), he begins "Back out of all this now too much for us" and ends "Drink and be whole again beyond confusion." The sixty lines between take us on a journey back in time, moving along an abandoned road, through what was once a village farm, to a brook from which we are invited to drink. On the way there we are asked to lose (and find) ourselves among lost places and the remnants of lost lives. But as much as the poem is an elegy for these, it is also a poem about the reading of poetry. The "all this now too much for us" is what we leave behind as we begin to read. This is the surfeited present, where the details of daily experience overwhelm us. It is the burgeoning commercial civilization spurned by Emerson and Thoreau, and it is today's consumer economy with its glittering overabundance. It is noise. What we drink, as we read, is the very opposite.

"Poetry," said Frost to a reporter in 1931, foreshadowing the movement of "Directive," "stands as a reminder of the rural life—as a resource, a recourse . . . We are now at a moment when we are getting too far out into the social-industrial and are at the point of drawing back—drawing in to renew ourselves." Renewing ourselves, for both Frost and Emerson, as well as Wordsworth, Shelley, and other poets of the Romantic movement, meant first and foremost the renewal of language; and renewing language meant returning to its roots. To do so one had to look first to the colloquial, where nouns were directly attached to objects and verbs to actions. This is what Emerson called "our ancient speech," a phrase from the poem "Monadnoc," which Frost often cited. "For that hardy English root," the poem continues, "Thrives here, unvalued, underfoot," suggesting something hidden underneath speech itself. For Emerson it was the "piquancy" in "the conversation of a strong-natured farmer or backwoodsman," and for Frost it was the lilt and thrust in the talk he heard around Derry, New Hampshire, and in what he called "the hard everyday word of the street."

Listening to that, and incorporating it in his poems, he developed a practical theory of poetry which he referred to variously in letters, interviews, and lectures as the "sentence-sound" or "sound of sense." Specifically, the overall sound of a spoken sentence conveys a meaning before its individual sounds are understood. Even when sound is separated from content, as for example in a conversation heard from behind a closed door, the nature of a sentence (declarative, interrogative, expletive, etc.), the emotion of the speaker, and various subtleties of feeling can be gathered simply from the tone, rhythm, pitch, and shape of speech. Poetry, without the implicit meaning and the freshness and verve of spoken language, is lifeless. Part of the trick then in writing a poem is to make sure that the sound of a sentence, as spoken, is built into the line. In Frost's words: "The actor's gift is to execute the vocal image at the mouth. The writer's is to implicate the vocal image in a sentence and fasten it to the page." This is exactly what he did, and more.

Rarely did he borrow sentences he heard and write them down verbatim. Rather he put together new sentences whose rhythms preserved and emphasized the speech patterns of the voice. He started doing this most directly with the dramatic dialogues in *North of Boston*. There, with no actors present, it was essential that the lines should sound spoken by living persons even when read silently.

> Off he goes always when I need him most.
> He thinks he ought to earn a little pay,
> Enough at least to buy tobacco with,
>
> (The Death of the Hired Man)

There is only one way to read these grumblings of a farmer over the absence of an old hired hand, and we are compelled to do so by the combination of meter and speech pattern. The meter is common iambic pentameter, the speech pattern no less familiar. They begin by working against each other, the speech pattern predominating. "Off he goes always when I need him most" can only be read with a stress on "Off," a lighter stress on "al-," and fairly substantial stresses on "need" and "most." The line would sound unnatural if read iambically, with stresses on "he" and every second syllable thereafter. But even when read normally the sentence still has enough meter to hold it solidly together, especially in the latter half. In the other two lines meter and speech pattern coincide so as to reinforce each other. Yet the speech pattern is complex enough to soften the effect of the iambic, so that these lines too are read with all the variety of spoken dialogue. A similar interplay occurs in lines uttered elsewhere by a door-to-door salesman, about his lackadaisical attitude toward working rural districts:

> I'm there, and they can pay me if they like.
> I go nowhere on purpose: I happen by.
>
> > (A Hundred Collars)

Frost composed such lines more or less spontaneously by ear, and they characterize his own laissez-faire approach: he let a poem find its own way and gradually happen, much as the traveling salesman by going nowhere on purpose would eventually arrive at somebody's doorstep. But when he worded the technique I have been describing he called it "breaking the sounds of sense with all their irregularity of accent across the regular beat of the metre"; and went on to say "I am never more pleased than when I get these into strained relation." Such balanced conflict, present in all the dialogues and in most of the shorter and longer lyrics from *North of Boston* on, gives his poetry its tension, and much of its humor and excitement, but the principle is hardly unique. One finds it especially in the plays of Shakespeare, which Frost had known since youth, and to a lesser extent in the lyrics of Wordsworth and other eighteenth- and nineteenth-century British poets with whom he was familiar. But Frost took it further than the latter, allowing himself more liberties. While maintaining an iambic base, he began easing blank and rhymed verse out of what was tending to become a metrical straitjacket. Just as Shakespeare had loosened up his meters with Elizabethan vernacular, Frost set against a traditionally iambic footing turns of phrase typical of New England.

The hard snow held me, save where now and then
One foot went through. The view was all in lines
Straight up and down of tall slim trees
Too much alike to mark or name a place by
So as to say for certain I was here
Or somewhere else: I was just far from home.

(The Wood-Pile)

"Save where," "name a place by, "say for certain" are so naturally imbedded in the iambic that we read right over them without singling them out as rural idioms. Yet they are, and they function far more effectively here than would a more formal equivalent. Apart from their concision, they help instill the passage with the very grain of the region, as in an old piece of wood well-polished by use. With "to mark or name a place by" the grain deepens into a sense of mystery, and in the long empty pause after "by," and in the lines that follow, mystery enlarges into a feeling of desolation. The pause is magical, as are the enjambments above and below, especially "The view was all in lines/Straight up and down of tall thin trees." But such magic did not come just out of thin air. It emerged from everything Frost had gathered from the whole tradition of English prosody with its many different musics and moods, combined with the fund of local language he had been storing away since the age of eleven. All this conspired with sheer invention to convey what Frost might have called the "vocal image" of the vast swamp his protagonist has entered.

> . . . I thought that only
Someone who lived in turning to fresh tasks
Could so forget his handiwork on which
He spent himself, the labor of his ax,
And leave it there far from a useful fireplace
To warm the frozen swamp as best it could
With the slow smokeless burning of decay.

(The Wood-Pile)

With the deceleration of "slow smokeless," the last line has the kind of classically smooth rhythmic closure that could easily have ended a poem by, say, a Keats or Shelley. But just above we have the colloquial "as best it could," whose sudden stop allows the line below to unwind like a long slow whip from a point of vocal tension. "And leave it there far from a useful fireplace" is altogether non-traditional, relaxing entirely out of the iambic to suggest the motion of someone already beginning to withdraw toward hearth and home. This and other, lesser relaxations give the passage the feel of informality. Yet the entire prolonged sentence of seven lines is a single integrated sound-shape, as skillfully put together as the abandoned wood-pile the speaker has come upon and will soon leave behind.

> His first thought under pressure was a grave
> In a new-boughten grave plot by herself,
> Under he didn't care how great a stone:
> He'd sell a yoke of steers to pay for it.
>
> (Place for a Third)

This shorter passage, equally composed, is full of colloquialism, almost comically juggled about. The juggling of syntax follows the actual sequence of events passing through the mind of a farmer contemplating (not so comically) a grave for his still-living wife. By imitating action, Frost's rearrangement of syntactical units draws all the images together into a single composite picture containing the graveyard, the purchase of the isolated plot, a stone of indeterminate size, and the yoked steers to be sold. Again and again Frost played with syntax in this way, always to make the picture more vivid and complete. Here is one portraying a half-wild colt trying to escape from his meadow:

> And now he comes again with clatter of stone,
> And mounts the wall again with whited eyes
> And all his tail that isn't hair up straight.
>
> (The Runaway)

And another:

> ...Bang goes something big away
> Off there upstairs.
>
> (In the Home Stretch)

And then from "Stopping by Woods on a Snowy Evening" there is the famous opening

> Whose woods these are I think I know.

This haunting sentence, and all the above passages, are only a few among countless realizations of the "vocal image." There is far more to it of course than that ghostlike hollowness of repeated o's, the juggling of syntax, or the juxtaposition of New England speech and traditional meter; and in the end the artistry or luck involved is difficult if not impossible to define. It may have something to do with the formation in the mind's eye of a fundamental sound-picture, a mental picture imbued with a sense of sound, and with contemplating that "vocal image" until nouns, verbs, and whole phrases come to mind that seem to harmonize with it visually and audibly. But whether the poem develops gradually or at once, the final product is often so strange as to resist analysis. The most one can do, in trying to understand its meanings and implications, is to let it lead the mind back to that basic picture, or to something similar. This is certainly one of the great pleasures of reading—for it opens the imagination to new territory. Rather than enlarging upon that, I simply want to say that Frost was one poet who really did, in his own words, "implicate the vocal image in a sentence and fasten it to the page." In so doing he achieved what Emerson had called for a half-century earlier when, railing against the continuing abstraction of language, he wrote that a true poet must "fasten words again to visible things."

Your Old Sweet-Cynical Strain

Fastening words to the visible meant reconnecting them to their roots in the natural world. For Emerson the origin and destination of poetry is always nature: it was from nature that language itself derived, eons ago, when human beings first began to name what they saw, and it is for poetry to reestablish the ancient primitive bond between object and word. Poetry should furthermore reawaken our sense of wonder: at the mystery of a single object, at the mystery of the universe entire. Finally, it should imply a relation between each individual object and the totality of things. In Emerson's terms true poetry sees that "there is no fact in nature which does not carry the whole sense of nature" and thus "reattaches things to nature and the Whole."

Up to this point Frost would agree, or mostly agree. There can be no doubt that his poetry is rooted in natural objects, that he looks on them with wonder, that his images have an aura of mystery hinting at something beyond the particular. But he and Emerson part company when it comes to what that something is. For Emerson, Thoreau, and the other transcendentalists, and for the Romantic movement in general, nature was *good*. It was infused with a divine benevolent presence which unified all things and conjoined them with humanity. It was the visible representation of a beneficent god or "oversoul"; and as such it was also the teacher of human conscience and morality, hence the source of all goodness in ourselves. For Frost, on the other hand, nature and humanity are ultimately apart, and nature itself is ambiguous, as frightening as it is beautiful. We may feel comfortable being in it, and we may love reaping from it, walking through its woods, and standing under its skies. But we are not necessarily loved in return. On the contrary, stones resist our plows, fire and flood destroy our shelters, and we are killed in the end by time and disease. What is most frightening, perhaps, is that there can be no blame. Nature is neither kind nor unkind. It seems to have nothing to do with us.

The Most of It

> He thought he kept the universe alone;
> For all the voice in answer he could wake
> Was but the mocking echo of his own

From some tree-hidden cliff across the lake.
Some morning from the boulder-broken beach
He would cry out on life, that what it wants
Is not its own love back in copy speech,
But counter-love, original response.
And nothing ever came of what he cried
Unless it was the embodiment that crashed
In the cliff's talus on the other side,
And then in the far distant water splashed,
But after a time allowed for it to swim,
Instead of proving human when it neared
And someone else additional to him,
As a great buck it powerfully appeared,
Pushing the crumpled water up ahead,
And landed pouring like a waterfall,
And stumbled through the rocks with horny tread,
And forced the underbrush—and that was all.

Emerson, Thoreau, and their European forebears woke us, fortunately, from the numbing effects of eighteenth-century rationalism. They revived our imagination, our intuition, our astonishment at the world, our innate mysticism, even our childlike pantheism, without which poetry would have remained, for a time at least, dry water. But in a traditional and primitivist way the Romantics reimposed upon nature and the universe a parental personality. No mother or father figure, however, inhabits this poem's landscape. There is neither human likeness nor any likeness at all. What Frost finds here is mute facelessness. The voice his lone protagonist once heard out of nature was nothing, he knows now, but his own echo from a cliff, and what he hopes is a sign of "counter-love" turns out to be a huge animal that snubs him, or worse, is not even aware of his presence. Yet there is no lack of awe on his part. If anything, the inhumanness of nature makes it seem all the more inexplicable and compelling.

The fading of a personality from nature marks the beginning of modern American poetry. Walt Whitman celebrated nature ecstatically, in long, free-verse poems which occasionally embellish it with human features, but its essence for him is formless and impersonal. In Emily Dickinson's poems nature is personified, but only as a poetic device, and nature itself remains for her an enigma. The depersonalization of nature has been accompanied by the gradual disappearance of rhyme and meter from the poetic line. Among the modern poets of New England, Frost and others continued to write in a relaxed iambic meter, rhymed or unrhymed, which still has its vital exponents; but what most are writing today is a free verse which at its finest is supplely and subtly shaped to its subject. Nature, from Dickinson to Frost to the present, is generally regarded with a mixture of puzzlement and distrust, usually understated, both translating into cautious respect:

The Need of Being Versed in Country Things

The house had gone to bring again
To the midnight sky a sunset glow.
Now the chimney was all of the house that stood,
Like a pistil after the petals go.

The barn opposed across the way,
That would have joined the house in flame
Had it been the will of the wind, was left
To bear forsaken the place's name.

No more it opened with all one end
For teams that came by the stony road
To drum on the floor with scurrying hoofs
And brush the mow with the summer load.

The birds that came to it through the air
At broken windows flew out and in,
Their murmur more like the sigh we sigh
From too much dwelling on what has been.

Yet for them the lilac renewed its leaf,
And the aged elm, though touched with fire;

And the dry pump flung up an awkward arm;
And the fence post carried a strand of wire.

For them there was really nothing sad.
But though they rejoiced in the nest they kept,
One had to be versed in country things
Not to believe the phoebes wept.

You could never convince a poor New Hampshire farmer that they did. Knowing from sore experience that the wind's will, if it had one, is capricious—that it blows in the phoebes' favor as often or as rarely as in ours—how could one believe they would feel any sympathy for us? Or feel anything at all, for that matter? Without thinking twice about it, they simply make a gain of our loss, perching where they can on what is left. Contemplating what was once a farm, Frost has taken an attitude here that is partly elegiac, partly tender, yet quietly skeptical. It is a tone captured by the phrase "Your old sweet-cynical strain" (from the poem "Voice Ways"), a tone typical of him in its equivocalness, and typical of the people he writes about. It speaks of a love for things of nature that is tempered by stony soil, long winters, and ever-changing weather. It emerges in language that is understated and economical, rhythms of speech that are subtle and subdued, and imagery that is neither overly dark nor overly bright or colorful. Briefly, it is a tone which always implies certain reservations, and so, on a cloudless summer morning, our New Hampshire farmer's only comment might be "almost nice out."

Such an unromantic though not indifferent view of nature is deeply ingrained in Frost's poems, as well as in those of his contemporaries, and is more or less constant in New England poetry up to and including the present. Nature is enjoyed, and quietly praised, sometimes with a certain rhapsody, but is never strictly good or evil, sympathetic, or antipathetic either. No matter if we desire a response, nature remains removed and inscrutable. Its distance from us is treated by some poets as an almost sacred fact of life, and its power over us is acknowledged and venerated. But by mid-century, and even before, that power is seen to be threatened. Frost himself speaks early on of the intrusion of train and telegraph, and later, of the challenge posed by the splitting of the atom; and more and more frequently now, in the poetry of New England and elsewhere, nature appears as vulnerable as ourselves. Polluted, deforested, and "developed," it is perceived more as our victim, today, than our oppressor.

Much of what I have just said about nature pertains to the poems in the first section of this book; the second has more to do with our individual being, within the nature that surrounds us and makes us wonder just who we are. Puritanism probably has something to do with the imperativeness of that question, and maybe the weather, too, puts a certain pressure on our skulls. Whatever the reason, our presence does not weigh lightly on us here, and so our poets tend to take it on with some persistence. Frost tried to deal with it by espousing an old-time rugged individualism endorsed by his reading of Emerson and Thoreau, among others, and personified, to a degree, in the farmers and mill-workers portrayed in his dramatic and narrative poems. Independent and hard-working, though generally either poor or simply getting by, these characters reflect in part the stoic, tight-lipped son of the soil that has become a New England archetype. None of them, however, not even the stubbornly male husband in "The Death of the Hired Man" or his counterpart in "Home Burial," is as self-contained and self-assured as one might expect. They may be wearing suits of armor, but there are chinks of sensitivity and self-doubt. The latter, especially, unable to commiserate with his wife over the death of their child, is painfully aware that he is trapped in his own maleness. In these poems and others Frost shows no small compassion for poorer farm women, as well as men, and particularly for their own poignant understanding of how much their lives are determined and restricted. A similar awareness is shown in the shorter, lyric poems whose speaker is observing his or her life and the "I" within it:

The Road Not Taken

Two roads diverged in a yellow wood,
And sorry I could not travel both
And be one traveler, long I stood
And looked down one as far as I could
To where it bent in the undergrowth;

Then took the other, as just as fair,
And having perhaps the better claim,
Because it was grassy and wanted wear;
Though as for that the passing there
Had worn them really about the same,

And both that morning equally lay
In leaves no step had trodden black.
Oh, I kept the first for another day!
Yet knowing how way leads on to way,
I doubted if I should ever come back.

I shall be telling this with a sigh
Somewhere ages and ages hence:
Two roads diverged in a wood, and I—
I took the one less traveled by,
And that has made all the difference.

Some have interpreted this poem as referring to Frost's own non-conformism: his refusal to travel the beaten path, his turning to farming and poetry, and his eventual literary triumph. It was read as a celebration of free will, choice, and individual enterprise. But there is no reason to believe that the poem is autobiographical, or is meant so positively. Underlying it is the question of what might have happened had I—?; and the resultant feeling is one of uncertainty, with more than a tinge of regret. Then there is the whole question of chance and contingency: how an apparently arbitrary choice leads to another and another, and so on, until one ends up in a kind of irreversible wandering. Finally there is the sense that one is lost within a labyrinth of roads, of ways haphazardly taken, and is somehow estranged from what one might call one's "life." This sense of lostness, similar to what haunts "The Woodpile" and "The Most of It," becomes more familiar the more of Frost you read. He gives it his own particular sound; but it is a keynote of modern poetry, the poetry of our region, and the poems included here, especially in section two.

There you will note that the self, as a concept, is increasingly subject to question. It is no longer seen as a clearly defined, islandlike thing enclosed in the cranium and confidently called "I" or "me." Rather it becomes intangible, its boundaries vague, its location uncertain. In this respect twentieth-century poetry reflects a similar tendency in other areas of thinking. Psychology has made us aware that each of us contains an immense unconscious which partially determines our behavior. Sociology has taught us that we are inseparable from history—from the political and economic conditions into which we are born. Science has shown us to be composed of particles of matter and energy in constant interchange with those of other entities. All this may seem limiting, for one can no longer consider oneself master of one's soul or king of one's castle. But it can just as well be liberating. The disintegration of the traditionally circumscribed self opens us to a much larger view of what it is to be in the world. We may feel lost in that view, but the sense of lostness that pervades much of this section need not be seen as negative. On the contrary, it may be a first step toward finding ourselves truly.

With section three, "Fences," we move from the individual to the sociopolitical. Direct engagement in the latter is a New England tradition, with a long history, from the war of independence to abolitionism to the labor movement and beyond. In fact the tactic known as "civil disobedience," often used in the civil rights and anti-war demonstrations of the 1960's, was formulated more than a century earlier by Thoreau, who was jailed for a night because of his refusal to pay a poll tax to a government that countenanced slavery and was waging war on Mexico. Poetry, too, might be considered a civilly disobedient act. Civil or uncivil, affirmative or negative, it tends to undermine the status quo. A well-made poem, like any highly formed artwork, tends to make whatever social order exists in the world outside it seem chaotic by comparison. Poetry furthermore can move us out of ourselves to a point where we can look beyond established institutions into other possibilities. Finally, there is a tradition in poetry, from as far back as the middle ages, of direct social criticism: criticism of the king, the church, the attitudes of a class or people, the policies of a state. The voice of the poet as social critic comes and goes from age to age, but it is strongly present in modern poetry, and no less in ours.

Frost, like Emerson and Thoreau, distrusted government, and his 1poetry shows it; generally however he preferred to keep his poems out of politics and away from direct criticism of society. Here and there you come across a poem that speaks out against war—the strongest being the "The Bonfire," with its bitterly ironic phrase "*War is for everyone, for children too.*" Then there are a few poems which deplore, not surprisingly, the encroachment of civilization on the rural landscape. The shrewdest of these, "A Brook in the City," tells of a farmhouse around which a city has built up, burying under streets the brook that once sustained both farm and farmer:

> . . . The brook was thrown
> Deep in a sewer dungeon under stone
> In fetid darkness still to live and run—
> And all for nothing it had ever done
> Except forget to go in fear perhaps.
> No one would know except for ancient maps
> That such a brook ran water. But I wonder
> If from its being kept forever under
> The thoughts may not have risen that so keep
> This new-built city from both work and sleep.

The suggestion is that the brook was paved over and imprisoned, not just for practical purposes, but because it was resented for its innocence of "fear." The poem implies that our so-called development of rural land is driven, at least in part, by envy. Nonetheless the unseen presence of the brook remains, under stone, to vex the city's inhabitants with intimations of something they know they have missed out on. Dungeoned, but not totally forgotten, it stays buried in their minds as an unconscious reminder of another life—a life unafraid, perhaps, of living *without* fear. It is the repressed memory of that other, freer way, and as such it is a hidden source of insomnia and anxiety. The poem is less about urbanization than about its alienating effect on the human psyche. With a handful of lines and one deep-going metaphor, it excavates its subject and explores its origins and consequences. Because it investigates a problem rather than simply attacking it, it is one of the more successful examples of social criticism in Frost's poetry.

There are other poems of Frost that yield a social or political meaning, usually by implication only. It is hard to consider the frozen marriages portrayed in "The Death of the Hired Man" or "Home Burial" without thinking of the kinds of change that might have thawed them out. Nor is it possible to read "Mending Wall" (the poem that begins section three) and fail to wonder what would happen if the wall were gone. Much of Frost's poetry honors the dignity of labor; and nearly all his poems reveal a deep regard for nature and one's fellow human beings—an attitude of care and care-taking which we can, if we wish, carry over into the political domain. But rarely do they engage social or political problems as directly as the work of other poets included in this section.

No one, Frost or anybody else, should feel obliged to turn their poetry in a sociopolitical direction, lest it become mere empty propaganda. Yet it is a fact that many, being haunted by history, plagued by what they see, have responded powerfully to the failing of government and society to meet an acceptable moral standard. Which is to say that they have responded to social wounds they feel acutely in themselves. Thus the negative response of many poems in this section is appropriate to its subject, whether it be war, the deterioration of cities, the violence of streets, material poverty, or poverty of spirit. Lurking behind their malaise is the sense that civilization is out of control, today perhaps more than ever, and that society, now, instead of nature, is an all-powerful force beyond our ability to tame. Such feelings are implicit in these poems, and some of them may be painful to read. But, by giving voice to the pain we feel, they help us recognize it for what it is and acknowledge its validity. By drawing attention to its causes, they help us get beyond it into something else.

What that something is remains unsaid, but the poems in the fourth and final section may hint at ways of approaching it. For Frost, the road there seems to be one that moves back into the rural past, away from the hustle of urban life, to a place that might once have been, or may never have been at all, except perhaps in poetry and in a past imagined. No less real for that, its landscape is one in which we find ourselves, as he says in the poem "Directive," by becoming "lost." Similarly, he sometimes spoke of his poetry as offering a kind of "threat." What I think he meant by that, and means in the poem, is that when we lose ourselves in poetry we lose our sense of separateness. We leave behind us a world of seemingly separate objects and enter one where things are integrated with each other and with ourselves. As word flows into word we have the impression that things are flowing one into the other. The world that evolves from them, continuous in its motion, is also continuous with *us*. At the same time its landscape keeps tempting us to go more deeply in, and the deeper we go the further its horizon opens. That seemingly limitless continuity, seductive as it is, contrasts so strongly with our more fragmentary everyday experience that we may feel discomforted. In this respect poetry may "threaten" our composure in the same way that the brook robs the city dwellers of their relative peace of mind. Yet poetry can also "save" us, as Frost said elsewhere, implying, I think, that it can give us a sense of true connectedness.

Frost's most often quoted definition of poetry is "a momentary stay against confusion." A momentary stay it is, but the rest of the phrase is questionable. Does the world outside the poem necessarily have to be one of permanent confusion? A portion of modern poetry assumes that it does, and even celebrates confusion, reveling or despairing in it as if it were a huge joke. But there is another kind of poetry that sees through confusion into the possibility of what I would call, for want of another word, community. I do not mean that the poems included here supply a formula for restructuring society. I mean that there is a communal way of thinking, a communal way of perceiving, in poetry that sees the most ordinary things as small miracles no more or less important than ourselves. Such poems look to a pair of common garden snakes, for example, or a squirrel, a pig, a cloud, sunlight on a city street, or the voice of a mower talking to his horses, as being in a sort of kinship with us in time. They imply, to quote a poem from elsewhere in the book, that "*we're in this together.*" Such a view suggests a way to live that is less conflicted, quieter, and more gentle than the aggressive and defensive behaviors that constitute our "fences." Skeptical of these, yet skeptical of any notion of divine unity or harmony, it suggests a reality which is nevertheless indivisible, unpossessable, and is a continuous source of puzzlement and wonder. In Emerson's words: "In our way of talking we say 'That is yours, this is mine'; but the poet knows well that it is not his; that it is as strange and beautiful to him as to you . . ."

But poems at least, Frost's or anyone else's, are ours to talk with, and I am thinking of community in that sense too. Language is itself communal, and poetry especially so. In reading a poem, as in talking with someone, we bring our lives to the words, just as the poet has brought an entire life to the writing of them. In order to understand, we try to live our way into that other life just as it lives its way into ours. Thus two lives merge, and if there are several of us reading a poem together then our lives too will come together as we speak of it. Though we can agree on meanings understood in common, the poem will live differently for each of us; and each of us will change and deepen, as poems themselves do, from one reading to the next.

A Time to Talk

When a friend calls to me from the road
And slows his horse to a meaning walk,
I don't stand still and look around
On all the hills I haven't hoed,
And shout from where I am, 'What is it?'
No, not as there is a time to talk.
I thrust my hoe in the mellow ground,
Blade-end up and five feet tall,
And plod: I go up to the stone wall
For a friendly visit.

I.

The Will of the Wind

Here, as already indicated in the introduction, are poems illustrating the changing perception of our place in the natural world. Initially we are seen as nature's prey, then eventually as nature's persecutor; and there are various gradations in between. Of the earlier view, Frost's well-known poem "An Old Man's Winter Night" is a prototype. There the wind-filled night bears down on a creaking farmhouse with universal weight, and all its lonely old tenant can do is light a lamp to keep away his fear. The farmer, his house, and the great "outer night" form a traditional hierarchy with the cosmos on top—a fundamental power structure inherent in such poems as Archibald MacLeish's "The Farm," Richard Eberhart's "Youth and Age," and Robert Penn Warren's "The Sky." In these poems and others, we human beings are small, our shelters frail, and both are totally subject to the forces of nature; and the wind, for one, carries with it a sense of infinite, frightening immensity.

Sometimes that immensity inspires less fear than awe. Implicit in Wallace Stevens's "The Snow Man" is a quiet agnostic marveling—a feeling that grows to affection, in Robert Francis's "The Reading of the Psalm," where an old woman looks out on a stormy night as into a familiar, well-loved text. Behind these and all the poems in this section lies an acknowledgment that nature is an incomprehensible mystery. That it is unknowable seems all the more reason to wonder at it, and indeed there are times when the response to that, as in Richard Wilbur's "An Event," is one of joy. Just as multitudes of small flying birds "roll," in that poem, "like a drunken fingerprint across the sky," so does the world happily escape all definition. Though momentarily captured in metaphor, none of it can really be held, nothing pinned down.

But civilization and industry have tried their level best to do so, often to the detriment of the environment. Worry about the latter creeps in here, beginning with William Meredith's "Country Stars." Then, with Maxine Kumin's "Noted in *The New York Times*" and Philip Booth's "Species," worry becomes fear for the very survival of animal and human life. Fear, in a passage from *Midsummer*, by Caribbean-born Derek Walcott, changes to a kind of weary disgust over the historic ruin he sees behind the touristic visage of Cape Cod. Sylvia Plath's "Green Rock, Winthrop Bay," sounds a requiem for a more urban segment of the coastline, depicted as a tar-stained eyesore, and a similar note can be heard in Brendan Galvin's poem "Pitch Pines," a devastatingly concise history of deforestation. Such poetry expresses the bitterness we feel when confronted with the disfigurement of a landscape we have loved and celebrated—a bitterness which Louise Gluck's "Witchgrass" turns to anger, namely nature's anger (uttered by the grass) against ourselves.

Yet there remains in many of these poems the sense that the land, in the end, will resist and that nature is as powerful as always. Indeed, the same hierarchy that appears in the Frost poem still holds true, not only for the nearly extinct subsistence farmer depicted in Galway Kinnell's "Farm Picture," but for the rest of us as well. Michael S. Harper's "The Drive In" makes it clear that New England weather, especially in winter, prevails over all, and so, in a sad, funny way, does Wesley McNair's "House in Spring." Nature, indifferently predatory in Linda Gregg's "The Copperhead," is benevolently life-giving in Jane

Kenyon's "August Rain, After Haying"; and in Margaret Gibson's "Long Walks in the Afternoon" it is as much a part of us as we who move in it are part of nature. Still, here and other places in this section, there is a feeling of cryptic secretiveness, as though something just beyond the visible were being withheld, something the "soul thirsts after," Kenyon observes, but "cannot name." Not limited to the rural, this same longing may be felt even in the city, as the closing poem, Martín Espada's "The Music of Astronomy," shows. There, as you will see, a flashlight beamed into the night's enigmatic silence is not so very different from the lamp held by Frost's ancient farmer.

Robert Frost

An Old Man's Winter Night

All out-of-doors looked darkly in at him
Through the thin frost, almost in separate stars,
That gathers on the pane in empty rooms.
What kept his eyes from giving back the gaze
Was the lamp tilted near them in his hand.
What kept him from remembering what it was
That brought him to that creaking room was age.
He stood with barrels round him—at a loss.
And having scared the cellar under him
In clomping here, he scared it once again
In clomping off; —and scared the outer night,
Which has its sounds, familiar, like the roar
Of trees and crack of branches, common things,
But nothing so like beating on a box.
A light he was to no one but himself
Where now he sat, concerned with he knew what,
A quiet light, and then not even that.
He consigned to the moon, such as she was,
So late-arising, to the broken moon
As better than the sun in any case
For such a charge, his snow upon the roof,
His icicles along the wall to keep;
And slept. The log that shifted with a jolt
Once in the stove, disturbed him and he shifted,
And eased his heavy breathing, but still slept.
One aged man—one man—can't keep a house,
A farm, a countryside, or if he can,
It's thus he does it of a winter night.

Wallace Stevens

The Snow Man

One must have a mind of winter
To regard the frost and the boughs
Of the pine-trees crusted with snow;

And have been cold a long time
To behold the junipers shagged with ice,
The spruces rough in the distant glitter

Of the January sun; and not to think
Of any misery in the sound of the wind,
In the sound of a few leaves,

Which is the sound of the land
Full of the same wind
That is blowing in the same bare place

For the listener, who listens in the snow,
And, nothing himself, beholds
Nothing that is not there and the nothing that is.

Archibald MacLeish

The Farm

Why do you listen, trees?
Why do you wait?
Why do you fumble at the breeze—
Gesticulate
With hopeless fluttering hands—
Stare down the vanished road beyond the gate
That now no longer stands?
Why do you wait—
Trees—
Why do you listen, trees?

(1750)

Ephraim Cross drives up the trail
From Worcester. Hepsibah goes pale
At sumac feathers in the pines.
The wooden wagon grunts and whines.
Blunt oxen leaning outward lurch
Over the boulders. Pine to birch
The hills change color. In the west
Wachusett humps a stubborn crest.
Ephraim takes the promised land,
Earth, rock and rubble, in his hand.

(1800)

Young sugar maples in a row
Flap awkward leaves. Ripe acres blow
In failing ripples to the blue
Of hemlocks. Ephraim's house stands true
Above the troubling of a brook.
Ephraim's gravestones seem to look
West of the Berkshires and still west.
Hepsibah's stones turn back compressed

And bitter silence toward the sea.
Between, her sons sleep patiently.

(1871)

A blind door yawing to the snow
Questions them in. They knock and go
Through the old bedroom to the back.
The kitchen door swings out a crack
Framing Aunt Aggie in her chair—
Dead as a haddock—ragged hair
Scrawled over on her shriveled eyes.
Since Monday morning, they surmise.
Last of her name she was, and best
Be lyin' up there with the rest.

(1923)

Plummets of moonlight thinning through
Deep fathoms of the dark renew
Moments of vision and deflect
Smooth images the eyes expect
To images the brain perceives.
Choked in a pine wood chafe the leaves
Of aged maples, but the moon
Remembers; and its shadows strewn
Sidelong and slantingly restore
Ephraim's trees about his door.

Why do you listen, trees?
Why do you wait?
Why do you fumble at the breeze—
Gesticulate
With hopeless fluttering hands—
Stare down the vanished road beyond the gate
That now no longer stands?
Why do you listen, trees?
Why do you listen, trees?

Robert Francis

The Reading of the Psalm

An old woman by a window watching the storm—
Dark river and dark sky and furious wind
Full of green flying leaves, gray flying rain.

Daughters and grandchildren in a darkened room
(The shutters closed, the shades drawn down)
Call to her to come, to come away.

Above the wind and the crash of a porch chair
And now the thunder, she does not seem to hear
Or if she hears, she does not answer them.

At the approach of storm she came upstairs
And closed her bedroom window. She stands there still,
Her hand resting upon the windowsill.

With eyes as calm, as unreproving, gentle
As though she watched the lighting of a candle
She watches how the lightning parts the sky.

Would she be safer were she not alone?
Would she be safer if the shades were drawn?
She does not ask. She does not think of safety.

Rather she thinks of deep roots drinking rain,
Of all dust washed from leaves, of pools filled,
Of cooler air and a good night for sleeping.

And if the lightning (while she stands there watching)
Touched her and closed her eyes— They are calling her
From the darkened room, "Mother, Grandmother, come!"

Slowly she turns away, having heard them call.
Turns from the storm as one might read a psalm
And look away and slowly close the book.

Richard Eberhart

Youth and Age

I remember when I was little and the world was great
A storm crashed the trees, lightnings vociferated,
Dark horror darkened the house, we descended
To the cellar in cold fear, in stupefying dread,
In wordless terror. I clung to the skirts of my mother.

Now I am old, and life continues, time is small.
Facing whatever may bring the end of the world
I have no better answer, now than then—
Blind clutches against the force of nature,
A wild glimpse, and poetry.

Robert Penn Warren

Sky

Livid to lurid switched the sky.
From west, from sunset, now the great dome
Arched eastward to lip the horizon edge,
There far, blank, pale. The grass, the trees,
Abandoned their kindly green to stretch
Into distance, arsenical now in that
Acid and arsenical light
Streaked yellow like urine.

                      Farmhouses afar—
They seemed to float, tiny and lost,
Swaying unmoored, forgotten in
That virulence past viridity
That washed, flooded, the world, and seemed
To lift all things, all houses, trees, hills,
From God-ordained foundations.

                           And
Your head in dizziness swam, while from
Southeast a blackness was towering
Toward you—sow-bellied, brute-nosed, coiling,
Twisting itself in pain, in rage,
And self-rage not yet discharged, and in
Its distant, sweeping downwardness
Uncentered pink flashes flickered pale but
In lethal promise. The sun's red eye
Now from western death glares.

                                              We,
We all, have much endured, buckling
Belts, hearts. Have borne the outrageous
And uncomprehended inclemencies—
Borne even against God's will, or fate's.
Some have survived. We fear, yes. But

What most we fear advances on
Tiptoe, breath aromatic. It smiles.

Its true name is what we never know.

Stanley Kunitz

The Image-Maker

A wind passed over my mind,
insidious and cold.
It is a thought, I thought,
but it was only its shadow.
Words came,
or the breath of my sisters,
with a black rustle of wings.
They came with a summons
that followed a blessing.
I could not believe
I too would be punished.
Perhaps it is time to go,
to slip alone, as at a birth,
out of this glowing house
where all my children danced.
Seductive Night! I have stood
at my casement the longest hour,
watching the acid wafer
of the moon slowly dissolving
in a scud of cloud, and heard
the farthest hidden stars
calling my name.
I listen, but I avert my ears
from Meister Eckhart's warning:
All things must be forsaken.
God scorns
to show Himself among images.

Constance Carrier

The Prospect Before Us

Someone on Walnut Hill has taken a picture,
reducing the town by distance to design
under an arch of sky whose empty vastness
the ample clouds can only underline.

All that is left of landscape lies at the bottom
of a sea of summer air: the town is drowned
under that sky, remote above the buildings
that in the picture scarcely clear the ground.

Yet when we look at it our gaze goes downward
to the landscape under those intangible seas:
we are intent to mark the South Church steeple,
or the railroad station, or one of the factories,

Willowbrook Park, or the highway off to Boston.
We are restless always until we identify
what we have known from another plane and angle.
A curious agitation drives the eye

to furnish the ego at once with reassurance,
establish bearings, prove our knowledge, find
here in a scene grown suddenly unfamiliar
some foothold for the orphaned anxious mind.

We must touch the earth, must seek a mortal solace,
must find ourselves, our own, our known, in the crowd,
before we can face the old inhuman spaces
above, before we can turn toward sky and cloud.

Elizabeth Bishop

Sandpiper

The roaring alongside he takes for granted,
and that every so often the world is bound to shake.
He runs, he runs to the south, finical, awkward,
in a state of controlled panic, a student of Blake.

The beach hisses like fat. On his left, a sheet
of interrupting water comes and goes
and glazes over his dark and brittle feet.
He runs, he runs straight through it, watching his toes.

—Watching, rather, the spaces of sand between them,
where (no detail too small) the Atlantic drains
rapidly backwards and downwards. As he runs,
he stares at the dragging grains.

The world is a mist. And then the world is
minute and vast and clear. The tide
is higher or lower. He couldn't tell you which.
His beak is focussed; he is preoccupied,

looking for something, something, something.
Poor bird, he is obsessed!
The millions of grains are black, white, tan, and gray,
mixed with quartz grains, rose and amethyst.

Robert Lowell

Water

It was a Maine lobster town—
each morning boatloads of hands
pushed off for granite
quarries on the islands,

and left dozens of bleak
white frame houses stuck
like oyster shells
on a hill of rock,

and below us, the sea lapped
the raw little match-stick
mazes of a weir,
where the fish for bait were trapped.

Remember? We sat on a slab of rock.
From this dance in time,
it seems the color
of iris, rotting and turning purpler,

but it was only
the usual gray rock
turning the usual green
when drenched by the sea.

The sea drenched the rock
at our feet all day,
and kept tearing away
flake after flake.

One night you dreamed
you were a mermaid clinging to a wharf-pile,
and trying to pull
off the barnacles with your hands.

We wished our two souls
might return like gulls
to the rock. In the end,
the water was too cold for us.

William Meredith

Country Stars

The nearsighted child has taken off her glasses
and come downstairs to be kissed goodnight.
She blows on a black windowpane until it's white.
Over the apple trees a great bear passes
but she puts her own construction on the night.

Two cities, a chemical plant, and clotted cars
breathe our distrust of darkness on the air,
clouding the pane between us and the stars.
But have no fear, or only proper fear:
the bright watchers are still there.

Hayden Carruth

The Loon on Forrester's Pond

Summer wilderness, a blue light
twinkling in trees and water, but even
wilderness is deprived now. "What's that?
What is that sound?" Then it came to me,
this insane song, wavering music
like the cry of the genie inside the lamp,
it came from inside the long wilderness
of my life, a loon's song, and there he was
swimming on the pond, guarding
his mate's nest by the shore,
diving and staying under
unbelievable minutes and coming up
where no one was looking. My friend
told how once in his boyhood
he had seen a loon swimming beneath his boat,
a shape dark and powerful
down in that silent world, and how
it had ejected a plume of white excrement
curving behind. "It was beautiful,"
he said.

The loon
broke the stillness over the water
again and again,
broke the wilderness

with his song, truly
a vestige, the laugh that transcends
first all mirth
and then all sorrow
and finally all knowledge, dying
into the gentlest quavering timeless
woe. It seemed
the real and only sanity to me.

Richard Wilbur

An Event

As if a cast of grain leapt back to the hand,
A landscapeful of small black birds, intent
On the far south, convene at some command
At once in the middle of the air, at once are gone
With headlong and unanimous consent
From the pale trees and fields they settled on.

What is an individual thing? They roll
Like a drunken fingerprint across the sky!
Or so I give their image to my soul
Until, as if refusing to be caught
In any singular vision of my eye
Or in the nets and cages of my thought,

They tower up, shatter, and madden space
With their divergences, are each alone
Swallowed from sight, and leave me in this place
Shaping these images to make them stay:
Meanwhile, in some formation of their own,
They fly me still, and steal my thoughts away.

Delighted with myself and with the birds,
I set them down and give them leave to be.
It is by words and the defeat of words,
Down sudden vistas of the vain attempt,
That for a flying moment one may see
By what cross-purposes the world is dreamt.

Alan Dugan

Note: The Sea Grinds Things Up

It's going on now
as these words appear
to you or are heard by you.
A wave slaps down, flat.
Water runs up the beach,
then wheels and slides
back down, leaving a ridge
of sea-foam, weed, and shells.
One thinks: I must
break out of this
horrible cycle, but
the ocean doesn't: it
continues through the thought.
A wave breaks, some
of its water runs up
the beach and down
again, leaving a ridge
of scum and skeletal debris.
One thinks: I must
break out of this
cycle of life and death,
but the ocean doesn't: it
goes past the thought.
A wave breaks on the sand,
water planes up the beach
and wheels back down,
hissing and leaving a ridge
of anything it can leave.
One thinks: I must
run out the life
part of this cycle,

then the death part
of this cycle, and then
go on as the sea
goes on in this cycle
after the last word,
but this is not the last
word unless you think
of this cycle as some
perpetual inventory
of the sea. Remember:
this is just one sea
on one beach on one
planet in one
solar system in one
galaxy. After that
the scale increases, so
this is not the last word,
and nothing else is talking back.
It's a lonely situation.

Maxine Kumin

Noted in *The New York Times*
Lake Buena Vista, Florida, June 16, 1987

Death claimed the last pure dusky seaside sparrow
today, whose coastal range was narrow,
as narrow as its two-part buzzy song.
From hummocks lost to Cape Canaveral
this mouselike skulker in the matted grass,
a six-inch bird, plain brown, once thousands strong,
sang *toodle-raeeee azhee,* ending on a trill
before the air gave way to rocket blasts.

It laid its dull white eggs (brown specked) in small
neat cups of grass on plots of pickleweed,
bulrushes, or salt hay. It dined
on caterpillars, beetles, ticks, the seeds
of sedges. Unremarkable
the life it led with others of its kind.

Tomorrow we can put it on a stamp,
a first-day cover with Key Largo rat,
Schaus swallowtail, Florida swamp
crocodile, and fading cotton mouse.
How simply symbols replace habitat!
The tower frames at Aerospace
quiver in the flush of another shot
where, once indigenous, the dusky sparrow
soared trilling twenty feet above its burrow.

Philip Booth

Species

For seasons beyond count, age
after age, through generations,
they watched us, naked of eye,

through every possible lens:
we were pictured, widely, as
of more or less intelligence.

They measured our migrations,
guessed at the code in our blood,
the tidal pull of the sun,

or what the stars told us.
In weather when we spoke clearly
what they only partially sensed,

they knew to tape our voices;
they collected how they thought
we spoke. Or sang. Of how

we spoke they wrote music.
To our habitats, fieldmarks, even
our habits of pairing, they made

themselves guides. They saw
in us an endangered species;
they listed us with governments.

Out of guilt for the hunting,
even long after, or for what
we barely reminded them of,

we believe they almost loved us.
What we can never know is
how we failed to let them feel

what we meant in our deepest instinct,
in the great dance of our silence.
At the latitudes where we winter,

we only know to gather, to sing
to our young and ourselves, warning
after warning of how they became extinct.

Galway Kinnell

Farm Picture

Black earth
turned up, clods
shining on their
western sides, hay
sprouting on top
of bales of spoiled
hay, an old
farmer bent far
over like *Australopithecus
robustus,* carrying two dented
pails of water out
to the hen yard.

Anne Sexton

Whale

Whale on the beach, you dinosaur,
what brought you smoothing into this dead harbor?
If you'd stayed inside you could have grown
as big as the Empire State. Still you are not a fish,
perhaps you like the land, you'd had enough of
holding your breath under water. What is it we want
of you? To take our warm blood into the great sea
and prove we are not the sufferers of God?
We are sick of babies crying and the birds flapping
loose in the air. We want the double to be big,
and ominous and we want to remember when you were
money in Massachusetts and yet were wild and rude
and killers. We want our killers dressed in black
like grease for we are sick of writing checks,
putting on our socks and working in the little boxes
we call the office.

Donald Hall

Names of Horses

All winter your brute shoulders strained against collars, padding
and steerhide over the ash hames, to haul
sledges of cordwood for drying through spring and summer,
for the Glenwood stove next winter, and for the simmering range.

In April you pulled cartloads of manure to spread on the fields,
dark manure of Holsteins, and knobs of your own clustered with
    oats.
All summer you mowed the grass in meadow and hayfield, the
mowing machine
clacketing beside you, while the sun walked high in the morning;

and after noon's heat, you pulled a clawed rake through the same
    acres,
gathering stacks, and dragged the wagon from stack to stack,
and the built hayrack back, up hill to the chaffy barn,
three loads of hay a day, hanging wide from the hayrack.

Sundays you trotted the two miles to church with the light load
of a leather quartertop buggy, and grazed in the sound of hymns.
Generation on generation, your neck rubbed the window sill
of the stall, smoothing the wood as the sea smooths glass.

When you were old and lame, when your shoulders hurt bending to
     graze,
one October the man who fed you and kept you, and harnessed you
     every morning,
led you through corn stubble to sandy ground above Eagle Pond,
and dug a hole beside you where you stood shuddering in your skin,

and lay the shotgun's muzzle in the boneless hollow behind your ear,
and fired the slug into your brain, and felled you into your grave,
shoveling sand to cover you, setting goldenrod upright above you,
where by next summer a dent in the ground made your monument.

For a hundred and fifty years, in the pasture of dead horses,
roots of pine trees pushed through the pale curves of your ribs,
yellow blossoms flourished above you in autumn, and in winter
frost heaved your bones in the ground—old toilers, soil makers:

O Roger, Mackerel, Riley, Ned, Nellie, Chester, Lady Ghost.

John Hollander

Grounds of Winter

The language of the howling wind allows an endless
Tale of winter to be told in one long syllable,
Here where this sea of flowing air has become a mere
Glaring of diffuse and mindless light, as unaware
As each dumb, chilling mid-day is of its transience,
Of how it will be grasped by the comprehensive dark.
Everything we see in such light is an optical
Allusion, and not to the winter of sunny noons,
Of smooth-packed snow gleaming in the farmyard, icicles
Eyeing the ground under the barn, of the white shed where
A dairymaid still churns by hand away at the tub
Of metaphor. Not to that, but to the fact-ridden
Land of the unfair cold space, of the unblinking time.

Derek Walcott

Midsummer: XXXI

Along Cape Cod, salt crannies of white harbors,
white spires, white filling stations, the orthodox
New England offering of clam-and-oyster bars,
like drying barnacles leech harder to their docks
as their day ebbs. Colonies of dark seamen,
whose ears were tuned to their earringed ancestors'
hymn of the Mediterranean's ground bass,
thin out like flocks of some endangered species,
their gutturals, like a parched seal's, on the rocks.
High on the hillsides, the crosstrees of pines
endure the Sabbath with the nerves of aspens.
They hear the Pilgrim's howl changed from the sibyl's,
that there are many nations but one God,
black hat, black-suited with his silver buckle,
damning the rock pool for its naiad's chuckle,
striking this coast with his priapic rod.
A chilling wind blows from my Methodist childhood.
The Fall is all around us—it is New England's
hellfire sermon, and my own voice grows hoarse in
the fog whose bellowing horn is the sea siren's:
a trawler groping from the Port of Boston,
snow, mixed with steam, blurring the thought of islands.

Sylvia Plath

Green Rock, Winthrop Bay

No lame excuses can gloss over
Barge-tar clotted at the tide-line, the wrecked pier
I should have known better.

Fifteen years between me and the bay
Profited memory, but did away with the old scenery
And patched this shoddy

Makeshift of a view to quit
My promise of an idyll. The blue's worn out:
It's a niggard estate,

Inimical now. The great green rock
We gave good use as ship and house is black
With tarry muck

And periwinkles, shrunk to common
Size. The cries of scavenging gulls sound thin
In the traffic of planes

From Logan Airport opposite.
Gulls circle gray under shadow of a steelier flight.
Loss cancels profit.

Unless you do this tawdry harbor
A service and ignore it, I go a liar
Gilding what's eyesore,

Or must take loophole and blame time
For the rock's dwarfed lump, for the drabbled scum,
For a churlish welcome.

Brendan Galvin

Pitch Pines

Some trees loft their heads
like symmetrical green bells,
but these, blown one-sided
by winds salted out of the northeast,
seem twisted from the germ.
Not one will lean the same way as another.

Knotted but soft, they mingle
ragged branches and rot to punkwood,
limbs flaking and dying
to ribs, to antlers and spidery twigs,
scaly plates slipping off the trunks.

Hanging on, oaks rattle maroon clusters
against winter. But these, resinous in flues,
blamed for a history of cellar holes,
snap in the cold and fall
to shapes like dragons asleep,

or thin out by dropping sour needles
on acid soil. For one week in May
they pollinate windows, a shower
that curdles water to golden scum.

From Bartholomew Gosnold's deck,
Brereton saw this cape timbered to its shores
with the hardwoods that fell to keels
and ribbing, to single meetinghouse beams
as long as eight men.

Stands of swamp cedar, cleared for cranberries,
were split to shakes or cut lengthwise
for foundations, while sheep cropped
elm and cherry sprouts
and plows broke the cleancut fields.

Fifty cords at a time, birch and maple
melted bog iron in pits; elm and beech
boiled the Atlantic to its salts; red oak
fired the glassworks at Sandwich—

till the desert floundered
out of the backlands and knocked
on the rear doors of towns
and this peninsula drifted
in brushfire haze,

and, clenching their cones
under crown fires, the grandfathers
of these pines held on until
heat popped their seeds
to the charred ground.

Charles Simic

Windy Evening

This old world needs propping up
When it gets this cold and windy.
The cleverly painted sets,
Oh, they're shaking badly!
They're about to come down.

There'll be nothing but infinite space then.
The silence supreme. Almighty silence.
Egyptian sky. Stars like torches
Of grave robbers entering the crypts of the kings.
Even the wind pausing, waiting to see.

Better grab hold of that tree, Lucille.
Its shape crazed, terror-stricken.
I'll hold the barn.
The chickens in it uneasy.
Smart chickens, rickety world.

Michael S. Harper

The Drive In

I drive west from the old dump,
ice booming, its layers
glistening patterns
in the minus air,
trees cracking under a load of ice.

The mink on the passenger floor,
who had quivered near the car door,
chased by dogs and snowmobiles,
unable to run in the high snow,
unable to feed in the ruddered woods,
stiffens on an old magazine.

I see a pelt and some food for a dog;
my VW made from war weaves
over the drifting snow; taken up
by the tail the mink's eyes widen,
headlights dimming in the high snow,
sounds of cracking ice booming—
sounds of driven, ruddered snow—

Wesley McNair

House in Spring

Where it stands in the wind
unpinning the plastic
it has worn all winter

there is not one tree,
and nobody sees the long
remnants unfolding

in the late light.
Now it is tossing them
across the windowless

pair of shutters
and the great, swollen
place in the clapboards.

Now it is drawing them back
from the stairless
front door again

and again like an old
burlesque queen, alone
in the potato fields

of Mars Hill, Maine.

Linda Gregg

The Copperhead

Almost blind he takes the soft dying
into the muscle-hole of his haunting.
The huge jaws eyeing, the raised head sliding
back and forth, judging the exact place of his killing.
He does not know his burden. He is not so smart.
He does not know his feelings. He only knows
his sliding and the changing of his hunger.
He waits. He sleeps. He looks but does not know his
seeing. He only knows the smallness of a moving.
He does not see the fear of the trapping.
He only sees the moving. He does not feel the caution.
He does not question. He only feels the flexing
and rearing of his wanting. He goes forward
where he is eyeing and knows the fastness
of his mouthing. He does not see the quickness collapsing.
He does not see at all what he has done. He only feels
the newness of his insides. The soft thing moving.
He does not see the moving. He is busy coaxing
and dreaming and feeling the softness moving in him.
The inside of him feels like another world.
He takes the soft thing and coaxes it
away from his small knowing. He would turn in and follow,
hunt it deep within the dark hall of his fading knowing,
but he cannot. He knows that.
That he cannot go deep within his body for the finding
of the knowing. So he slows and lets go. And finds
with his eyes a moving. A small moving that he knows.

Louise Gluck

Witchgrass

Something
comes into the world unwelcome
calling disorder, disorder—

If you hate me so much
don't bother to give me
a name: do you need
one more slur
in your language, another
way to blame
one tribe for everything—

as we both know,
if you worship
one god, you only need
one enemy—

I'm not the enemy.
Only a ruse to ignore
what you see happening
right here in this bed,
a little paradigm
of failure. One of your precious flowers
dies here almost every day
and you can't rest until
you attack the cause, meaning
whatever is left, whatever
happens to be sturdier
than your personal passion—

It was not meant
to last forever in the real world.
But why admit that, when you can go on
doing what you always do,
mourning and laying blame,
always the two together.

I don't need your praise
to survive. I was here first,
before you were here, before
you ever planted a garden.
And I'll be here when only the sun and moon
are left, and the sea, and the wide field.

I will constitute the field.

Margaret Gibson

Long Walks in the Afternoon

Last night the first light frost, and now sycamore
and sumac edge yellow and red in low sun
and indian afternoons. One after another

roads thicken with leaves and the wind
sweeps them fresh as the start of a year.
A friend writes she is tired of being one

on whom nothing is lost, but what choice
is there, how can she close her eyes?
I walk for hours—either

with hands behind my back like a prisoner,
neck craning up to the sky where chain gang
birds in tight nets

fly south—or with hands swinging free at my sides
to the brook, the water so cold it stings
going down. Either way, I whisper

to dogwood, fern, stone walls, and the last
mosquito honing in, *we're in this together.*
Here is the road. Honest dirt

and stone. Some afternoon, heading home before dark,
if I walk by mistake, lost in thought, far beyond
the steep trees, the satellites and stars,

up over the rim to a pitfall, past any memory of words—
even then I can give my body its lead,
still find my way back.

Jane Kenyon

August Rain, after Haying

Through sere trees and beheaded
grasses the slow rain falls.
Hay fills the barn; only the rake
and one empty wagon are left
in the field. In the ditches
goldenrod bends to the ground.

Even at noon the house is dark.
In my room under the eaves
I hear the steady benevolence
of water washing dust
raised by the haying
from porch and car and garden
chair. We are shorn
and purified, as if tonsured.

The grass resolves to grow again,
receiving the rain to that end,
but my disordered soul thirsts
after something it cannot name.

Martín Espada

The Music of Astronomy

Every night
the ex-mental patient,
forgetful of the medicine
that caused him to forget,
would climb to the roof
of the transient hotel
with a flashlight,
waiting for his Martian parents
and their spaceship,
flashlight beam waving
like the baton of a conductor
firm in the faith
that this orchestra
will one night
give him music.

II.

My Own Desert Places

In this section the poets turn their gaze from the sky, the cosmos, and the visible world to the inner space of the psyche. In Frost's "Desert Places" all it contains is a feeling of emptiness brought on by the sight of a barren winter field. In Warren's "Better Than Counting Sheep" it is a mind half-remembering its past, whose nameless figures sweep away any sense of personal identity. In Stanley Kunitz's "Quinnapoxet" it is the subconscious mind experiencing a dream, perhaps a recurrent one, of the poet's mother and the father whom he never knew. All three poems place their speakers at a distance from exterior reality, rendering them strange to themselves and their surroundings. Similarly, and a little comically, Elizabeth Bishop, in her poem "In the Waiting Room," recalls from her childhood the moment when she first became aware of how very odd it is to be a living, conscious person.

The feeling of "lostness" pervading these poems is expressed more directly in Hayden Carruth's poem titled with almost the same word. Replying to Frost's "The Road Not Taken," Carruth begins "Many paths in the woods have chosen me . . . " and in looking back on life concludes that "losing and finding were the same." Taking the Frost poem a step further, he comes to the realization that he has found himself by yielding to the randomness of life and by admitting and accepting uncertainty. The latter, in Philip Booth's "Supposition with Qualification," is seen as a desirable, even ideal, way for us to receive experience: by open-mindedly and openhandedly accepting each moment as it is given. Instead of forcing it to become what we desire, we would simply let the moment be, apprehending it "in its own light" rather than ours; and with that we might, like Galway Kinnell in "The Room," briefly enter a space of time that seems to open on eternity. The poem in these instances is seen as a form of meditation, resulting in a relaxation of the will and a corresponding enlargement and deepening of vision.

Yet our individual identities, personalities, and public and professional roles tend to get in the way of that. We may shed them at night, as Charles Simic does with "Shirt," and have a tortuous time climbing back into them in the morning. Or we may yearn to leave them behind, escaping out the back window, like Alan Dugan in "Not to Choose." Or we may dream of dropping out altogether, like Wakeville in Donald Hall's "Mr. Wakeville on Interstate 90," and hiding away somewhere in a comfortingly fictitious life. But identity, shunned or not, is inescapable. It is, as Constance Carrier suggests in "Perspective," a necessary fiction, "however much it lies." It is a shape we have to have, and though it may oversimplify what is out there, it provides us with a needed lens. It also saves us from drowning in the subconscious—the sort of shapelessness which, in John Hollander's "The Angler's Story," burbles up from under. In short, it gives us a form for psychological, if not physical, survival.

But identity can suffocate us nonetheless, as happens to some of the figures portrayed here. The fathers, for example, in Kumin's "My Father's Neckties" and Anne Sexton's "Santa," are both in disguise, figuratively or literally, and hiding behind burlesque masks that conceal their true emotions, probably from themselves as much as their children. Men of their generation were required, of course, to keep their feelings under wraps. They also had to appear masterful; and this may well be why the father in Sylvia Plath's "The Colossus" is so enormous. He stands there a huge ruined monument, possibly broken during his lifetime, just as the father in Sexton's poem, inside his Santa Claus outfit, is pitifully alcoholic. Both were presumably under pressure to maintain a respectable level of financial security; and presumably these fathers did—but at what cost? And what about those who fail, as happens to a poorer man, under heavier pressure, in Espada's "The Toolmaker Unemployed?" They can easily end up losing all self-esteem and feeling as empty as the toolmaker's wallet.

Robert Frost

Desert Places

Snow falling and night falling fast, oh, fast
In a field I looked into going past,
And the ground almost covered smooth in snow,
But a few weeds and stubble showing last.

The woods around it have it—it is theirs.
All animals are smothered in their lairs.
I am too absent-spirited to count;
The loneliness includes me unawares.

And lonely as it is that loneliness
Will be more lonely ere it will be less—
A blanker whiteness of benighted snow
With no expression, nothing to express.

They cannot scare me with their empty spaces
Between stars—on stars where no human race is.
I have it in me so much nearer home
To scare myself with my own desert places.

Wallace Stevens

Less and Less Human, O Savage Spirit

If there must be a god in the house, must be,
Saying things in the rooms and on the stair,

Let him move as the sunlight moves on the floor,
Or moonlight, silently, as Plato's ghost

Or Aristotle's skeleton. Let him hang out
His stars on the wall. He must dwell quietly.

He must be incapable of speaking, closed,
As those are: as light, for all its motion, is;

As color, even the closest to us, is;
As shapes, though they portend us, are.

It is the human that is the alien,
The human that has no cousin in the moon.

It is the human that demands his speech
From beasts or from the incommunicable mass.

If there must be a god in the house, let him be one
That will not hear us when we speak: a coolness,

A vermilioned nothingness, any stick of the mass
Of which we are too distantly a part.

Archibald MacLeish

The Old Gray Couple

They have only to look at each other to laugh—
no one knows why, not even they:
something back in the lives they've lived,
something they both remember but no words can say.

They go off at an evening's end to talk
but they don't, or to sleep but they lie awake—
hardly a word, just a touch, just near,
just listening but not to hear.

Everything they know they know together—
everything, that is, but one:
their lives they've learned like secrets from each other;
their deaths they think of in the nights alone.

Robert Francis

Identity

This human footprint stamped in the moist sand
Where the mountain trail crosses the mountain brook
Halts me as something hard to understand.
I look at it with half-incredulous look.

Can this step pointing up the other way
Be one that I made here when I passed by?
This step detached and old as yesterday—
Can it be mine, my step? Can it be I?

Richard Eberhart

'If I could only live at the Pitch that is near Madness'

If I could only live at the pitch that is near madness
When everything is as it was in my childhood
Violent, vivid, and of infinite possibility:
That the sun and the moon broke over my head.

Then I cast time out of the trees and fields,
Then I stood immaculate in the Ego;
Then I eyed the world with all delight,
Reality was the perfection of my sight.

And time has big handles on the hands,
Fields and trees a way of being themselves.
I saw battalions of the race of mankind
Standing stolid, demanding a moral answer.

I gave the moral answer and I died
And into a realm of complexity came
Where nothing is possible but necessity
And the truth wailing there like a red babe.

Robert Penn Warren

Better Than Counting Sheep

For a night when sleep eludes you, I have,
At last, found the formula. Try to summon

All those ever known who are dead now, and soon
It will seem they are there in your room, not chairs enough

For the party, or standing space even, the hall
Chock-full, and faces thrust to the pane to peer.

Then somehow the house, in a wink, isn't there,
But a field full of folk, and some,

Those near, touch your sleeve, so sadly and slow, and all
Want something of you, too timid to ask—and you don't

Know what. Yes, even in distance and dimness, hands
Are out—stretched to glow faintly

Like fox-fire in marshland where deadfall
Rots, though a few trunks unsteadily stand.

Meanwhile, in the grieving susurrus, all wordless,
You sense, at last, what they want. Each,

Male or female, young or age-gnawed, beloved or not—
Each wants to know if you remember a name.

But now you can't answer, not even your mother's name, and your
  heart
Howls with the loneliness of a wolf in

The depth of a snow-throttled forest when the moon, full,
Spills the spruce-shadows African black. Then you are, suddenly,

Alone. And your own name gone, as you plunge in ink-shadow or
  snowdrift.
The shadows are dreams—but of what? And the snowdrift, sleep.

Stanley Kunitz

Quinnapoxet

I was fishing in the abandoned reservoir
back in Quinnapoxet,
where the snapping turtles cruised
and the bullheads swayed
in their bower of tree-stumps,
sleek as eels and pigeon-fat.
One of them gashed my thumb
with a flick of his razor fin
when I yanked the barb
out of his gullet.
The sun hung its terrible coals
over Buteau's farm: I saw
the treetops seething.

They came suddenly into view
on the Indian road,
evenly stepping
past the apple orchard,
commingling with the dust
they raised, their cloud of being,
against the dripping light
looming larger and bolder.
She was wearing a mourning bonnet
and a wrap of shining taffeta.
"Why don't you write?" she cried
from the folds of her veil.

"We never hear from you."
I had nothing to say to her.
But for him who walked behind her
in his dark worsted suit,
with his face averted
as if to hide a scald,
deep in his other life,
I touched my forehead
with my swollen thumb
and splayed my fingers out—
in deaf-mute country
the sign for father.

Constance Carrier

Perspective

You see these images
   existing but to prove
your own identity,
   your single self, who move
among them, and you say
   The presence of this door,
my shadow on this wall,
   this window and this light
reflect me to myself
   and make my stature more,
my self more surely right
   who walk here in the night.

I by another way
   have come to the same end:
here from the small hill's height
   I stare across the plain:
against a leaf I measure
   the mile-diminished town,
and say, It is my sight
   that has arranged this scene:
my sight alone decrees
   the height of spire and trees:
my eyes may at their pleasure,
   my heart may at its will,
reduce, exaggerate,
   refute the actual:

and these distortions—not
    to be escaped from ever,
as once I hoped and thought—
    are part and proof of me,
spring from my heart and eyes
    to prove the self secure
however much it lies.

Elizabeth Bishop

In the Waiting Room

In Worcester, Massachusetts,
I went with Aunt Consuelo
to keep her dentist's appointment
and sat and waited for her
in the dentist's waiting room.
It was winter. It got dark
early. The waiting room
was full of grown-up people,
arctics and overcoats,
lamps and magazines.
My aunt was inside
what seemed like a long time
and while I waited I read
the *National Geographic*
(I could read) and carefully
studied the photographs:
the inside of a volcano,
black, and full of ashes;
then it was spilling over
in rivulets of fire.
Osa and Martin Johnson
dressed in riding breeches,
laced boots, and pith helmets.
A dead man slung on a pole
—"Long Pig," the caption said.
Babies with pointed heads
wound round and round with string;
black, naked women with necks
wound round and round with wire
like the necks of light bulbs.
Their breasts were horrifying.

I read it right straight through.
I was too shy to stop.
And then I looked at the cover:
the yellow margins, the date.

Suddenly, from inside,
came an *oh!* of pain
— Aunt Consuelo's voice —
not very loud or long.
I wasn't at all surprised;
even then I knew she was
a foolish, timid woman.
I might have been embarrassed,
but wasn't. What took me
completely by surprise
was that it was *me:*
my voice, in my mouth.
Without thinking at all
I was my foolish aunt,
I—we—were falling, falling,
our eyes glued to the cover
of the *National Geographic,*
February, 1918.

I said to myself: three days
and you'll be seven years old.
I was saying it to stop
the sensation of falling off
the round, turning world
into cold, blue-black space.
But I felt: you are an *I,*
you are an *Elizabeth,*
you are one of *them.*
Why should you be one, too?
I scarcely dared to look
to see what it was I was.

I gave a sidelong glance
—I couldn't look any higher—
at shadowy gray knees,
trousers and skirts and boots
and different pairs of hands
lying under the lamps.
I knew that nothing stranger
had ever happened, that nothing
stranger could ever happen.
Why should I be my aunt,
or me, or anyone?
What similarities—
boots, hands, the family voice
I felt in my throat, or even
the *National Geographic*
and those awful hanging breasts—
held us all together
or made us all just one?
How—I didn't know any
word for it—how "unlikely". . .
How had I come to be here,
like them, and overhear
a cry of pain that could have
got loud and worse but hadn't?

The waiting room was bright
and too hot. It was sliding
beneath a big black wave,
another, and another.

Then I was back in it.
The War was on. Outside,
in Worcester, Massachusetts,
were night and slush and cold,
and it was still the fifth
of February, 1918.

Robert Lowell

For Sale

Poor sheepish plaything,
organized with prodigal animosity,
lived in just a year—
my Father's cottage at Beverly Farms
was on the market the month he died.
Empty, open, intimate,
its town-house furniture
had an on tiptoe air
of waiting for the mover
on the heels of the undertaker.
Ready, afraid
of living alone till eighty,
Mother mooned in a window,
as if she had stayed on a train
one stop past her destination.

William Meredith

Parents

for Vanessa Meredith and Samuel Wolf Gezari

What it must be like to be an angel
or a squirrel, we can imagine sooner.

The last time we go to bed good,
they are there, lying about darkness.

They dandle us once too often,
these friends who become our enemies.

Suddenly one day, their juniors
are as old as we yearn to be.

They get wrinkles where it is better
smooth, odd coughs, and smells.

It is grotesque how they go on
loving us, we go on loving them.

The effrontery, barely imaginable,
of having caused us. And of how.

Their lives: surely
we can do better than that.

This goes on for a long time. Everything
they do is wrong, and the worst thing,

they all do it, is to die,
taking with them the last explanation,

how we came out of the wet sea
or wherever they got us from,

taking the last link
of that chain with them.

Father, mother, we cry, wrinkling,
to our uncomprehending children and grandchildren.

Hayden Carruth

Lost

Many paths in the woods have chos-
    en me, many a time,
and I wonder often what this
    choosing is: a sublime

intimation from far outside
    my consciousness (or for
that matter from far inside) or
    maybe some train of mor-

tality set in motion at
    my birth (if our instru-
ments of observation were fine
    and precise enough to

trace it) or maybe only dis-
    parate appeal, pure chance,
the distant drumming of a par-
    tridge in spring, the advanc-

ing maple-color along a
    lane in fall, or only
that the mud was less thick one way
    than another was. Free

or determined? Again and a-
    gain I went the one way
and not the other, who knows why?
    I wish I could know. May-

be it would explain the other
    things that worry me. But
I have no compulsive need now,
    not any longer. What

I know is that whether I walked
  freely or trudged exhaust-
ed I chose one way each time and
  ended by being lost.

I think I sought it. I think I
  could not know myself un-
til I did not know where I was.
  Then my self-knowledge con-

tinued for a while while I found
  my way again in fear
and reluctance, lost truly at
  last. I changed the appear-

ance of myself to myself
  continually and
losing and finding were the same,
  as now I understand.

Richard Wilbur

In Limbo

What rattles in the dark? The blinds at Brewster?
I am a boy then, sleeping by the sea,
Unless that clank and chittering proceed
From a bent fan-blade somewhere in the room,
The air-conditioner of some hotel
To which I came too dead-beat to remember.
Let me, in any case, forget and sleep.
But listen: under my billet window, grinding
Through the shocked night of France, I surely hear
A convoy moving up, whose treads and wheels
Trouble the planking of a wooden bridge.

For a half-kindled mind that flares and sinks,
Damped by a slumber which may be a child's,
How to know when one is, or where? Just now
The hinged roof of the Cinema Vascello
Smokily opens, beaming to the stars
Crashed majors of a final panorama,
Or else that spume of music, wafted back
Like a girl's scarf or laughter, reaches me
In adolescence and the Jersey night,
Where a late car, tuned in to wild casinos,
Guns past the quiet house towards my desire.

Now I could dream that all my selves and ages,
Pretenders to the shadowed face I wear,
Might, in this clearing of the wits, forgetting
Deaths and successions, parley and atone.
It is my voice which prays it; mine replies
With stammered passion or the speaker's pause,
Rough banter, slogans, timid questionings—
Oh, all my broken dialects together;

And that slow tongue which mumbles to invent
The language of the mended soul is breathless,
Hearing an infant howl demand the world.

Someone is breathing. Is it I? Or is it
Darkness conspiring in the nursery corner?
Is there another lying here beside me?
Have I a cherished wife of thirty years?
Far overhead, a long susurrus, twisting
Clockwise or counterclockwise, plunges east,
Twin floods of air in which our flagellate cries,
Rising from love-bed, childbed, bed of death,
Swim toward recurrent day. And farther still,
Couched in the void, I hear what I have heard of,
The god who dreams us, breathing out and in.

Out of all that I fumble for the lamp-chain.
A room condenses and at once is true—
Curtains, a clock, a mirror which will frame
This blinking mask the light has clapped upon me.
How quickly, when we choose to live again,
As Er once told, the cloudier knowledge passes!
I am a truant portion of the all
Misshaped by time, incorrigible desire
And dear attachment to a sleeping hand,
Who lie here on a certain day and listen
To the first birdsong, homelessly at home.

Alan Dugan

Not to Choose

I should be someplace else!,
but pace around in the sweats
of inhumane endeavor and its trash:
goods, deeds, credits, debts.
Have it your own way, life:
I'm just here to die, but I
would rather live it out as a fool
and have a short life in contempt
and idle graces, but, instead,
the office telephone goes off
and voices out of its dark night
command me, "Choose, Choose,"
while women's angel voices call
the cities and their numbers. Then,
when I do choose: "I run away!"
the shop door opens and a cop
or statue stands there in the way.
What does he want? Blood. Oh
let me tumble in the wards, bolts,
and chambers of a police lock locked
so I can get to sleep again,
warm in the guaranteed steel!
Instead, I have to fake him off
with promises to pay. Cash!
How cold action is. I should
do spiritual exercises toward
the body of this world
and get in shape for choices,

choices, No! Instead, I leave
the dirty business by the back
window, climb down the fire escape,
and sneak off out of town alive
with petty cash and bad nerves in
an old Ford with a broken muffler!
So here I am again, July,
vacationing in your country broke,
in debt, not bankrupt yet!
and free to get your message!
What is it?
To begin again in another state!

Maxine Kumin

My Father's Neckties

Last night my color-blind chainsmoking father
who has been dead for fourteen years
stepped up out of a basement tie shop
downtown and did not recognize me.

The number he was wearing was as terrible
as any from my girlhood, a time of
ugly ties and acrimony: six or seven
blue lightning bolts outlined in yellow.

Although this was my home town it was tacky
and unfamiliar, it was Rabat or Gibraltar
Daddy smoking his habitual
square-in-the-mouth cigarette and coughing
ashes down the lightning jags. He was
my age exactly, it was wordless, a window
opening on an interior we both knew
where we had loved each other, keeping it quiet.

Why do I wait years and years to dream this outcome?
My brothers, in whose dreams he must as surely
turn up wearing rep ties or polka dots clumsily
knotted, do not speak of their encounters.

When we die, all four of us, in
whatever sequence, the designs
will fall off like face masks
and the rayon ravel from this hazy version
of a man who wore hard colors recklessly
and hid out in the foreign
bargain basements of his feelings.

Philip Booth

Supposition with Qualification

If he could say it, he meant to.
Not what it meant, if he ever knew,

but how it felt when he let himself
feel—even afraid of himself—

yet in that moment opened
himself to how the moment happened.

He meant to give himself up:
to how it could be when he gave up

requiring that each event shape
itself to his shape, his hope,

and intent. He meant not to weigh it,
whatever happened; only to let it

balance in its own light, to let light
fall where it would. If he could say it.

Galway Kinnell

The Room

The door closes on pain and confusion.
The candle flame wavers from side to side
as though trying to break itself in half
to color the shadows too with living light.
The andante movement plays over and over
its many triplets, like farm dogs yapping
at a melody made of the gratification-cries
of cocks. I will not stay long.
Nothing in experience led me to imagine
having. Having is destroying, said
my version of the vow of impoverishment.
But here, in this brief, waxen light,
I have, and nothing is destroyed. The flute
that guttered those owl's notes into the waste hours
of childhood joins with the piano
and they play, *Being is having.* Having
may be nothing but the grace of the shell
moving without hesitation, with lively pride,
down the stubborn river of woe. At the far end,
a door no one dares open begins opening.
To go through it will awaken such regret
as only closing it behind can obliterate.
The candle flame's staggering makes the room
wobble and shift—matter itself, laughing.
I can't come back. I won't change.
I have the usual capacity for wanting
what may not even exist. Don't worry.
That is the dew wetting my face.
You see? Nothing that enters the room
can have only its own meaning ever again.

Anne Sexton

Santa

Father,
the Santa Claus suit
you bought from Wolff Fording Theatrical Supplies,
back before I was born,
is dead.
The white beard you fooled me with
and the hair like Moses,
the thick crimpy wool
that used to buzz me on the neck,
is dead.
Yes, my busting rosy Santa,
ringing your bronze cowbell.
You with real soot on your nose
and snow (taken from the refrigerator some years)
on your big shoulder.
The room was like Florida.
You took so many oranges out of your bag
and threw them around the living room,
all the time laughing that North Pole laugh.
Mother would kiss you
for she was that tall.
Mother could hug you
for she was not afraid.
The reindeer pounded on the roof.
(It was my Nana with a hammer in the attic.
For *my* children it was my husband
with a crowbar breaking things up.)
The year I ceased to believe in you
is the year you were drunk.

My boozy red man,
your voice all slithery like soap,
you were a long way from Saint Nick
with Daddy's cocktail smell.
I cried and ran from the room
and you said, "Well, thank God that's over!"
And it was, until the grandchildren came.
Then I tied up your pillows
in the five A.M. Christ morning
and I adjusted the beard,
all yellow with age,
and applied rouge to your cheeks
and Chalk White to your eyebrows.
We were conspirators,
secret actors,
and I kissed you
because I was tall enough.
But that is over.
The era closes
and large children hang their stockings
and build a black memorial to you.
And you, you fade out of sight
like a lost signalman
wagging his lantern
for the train that comes no more.

Donald Hall

Mr. Wakeville on Interstate 90

"Now I will abandon the route of my life
as my shadowy wives abandon me, taking my children.
I will stop somewhere. I will park in a summer street
where the days tick like metal in the stillness.
I will rent the room over Bert's Modern Barbershop
where the TO LET sign leans in the plateglass window;
or I will buy the brown BUNGALOW FOR SALE.

"I will work forty hours a week clerking at the paintstore.
On Fridays I will cash my paycheck at Six Rivers Bank
and stop at Harvey's Market and talk with Harvey.
Walking on Maple Street I will speak to everyone.
At basketball games I will cheer for my neighbors' sons.
I will watch my neighbors' daughters grow up, marry,
raise children. The joints of my fingers will stiffen.

"There will be no room inside me for other places.
I will attend funerals regularly and weddings.
I will chat with the mailman when he comes on Saturdays.
I will shake my head when I hear of the florist
who drops dead in the greenhouse over a flat of pansies;
I spoke with her only yesterday.
When lawyer elopes with babysitter I will shake my head.

"When Harvey's boy enlists in the Navy
I will wave goodbye at the Trailways depot with the others.
I will vote Democratic; I will vote Republican.
I will applaud the valedictorian at graduation
and wish her well as she goes away to the university
and weep as she goes away. I will live in a steady joy;
I will exult in the ecstasy of my concealment."

John Hollander

The Angler's Story

I let down my long line; it went falling; I pulled. Up came
A bucket of bad sleep in which tongues were sloshing about
Like frogs and dark fish, breaking the surface of silence, the
Forgetfulness, with what would have been brightness in any
Other element, flash of wave, residual bubbling,
But were here belches of shadow churned up by the jostling
Tongues from the imageless thick bottom of the heavy pail.
I could not reach into that fell stuff after them, nor fling
Them back into night like inadequate fish; nor would they
Lie flat and silent like sogged leaves that had been flung under
Mud, but burbled of language too heavy to be borne, of
Drowned inflections and smashed predications, exactness pulped
Into an ooze of the mere desire to utter. It was
My bucket, and I have had to continue to listen.

Derek Walcott

For Adrian

> *April 14, 1986*
> *To Grace, Ben, Judy, Junior, Norline,*
> *Katryn, Gem, Stanley, and Diana*

Look, and you will see that the furniture is fading,
that a wardrobe is as insubstantial as a sunset,

that I can see through you, the tissue of your leaves,
the light behind your veins; why do you keep sobbing?

The days run through the light's fingers like dust
or a child's in a sandpit. When you see the stars

do you burst into tears? When you look at the sea
isn't your heart full? Do you think your shadow

can be as long as the desert? I am a child, listen,
I did not invite or invent angels. It is easy

to be an angel, to speak now beyond my eight years,
to have more vestal authority, and to know,

because I have now entered a wisdom, not a silence.
Why do you miss me? I am not missing you, sisters,

neither Judith, whose hair will banner like the leopard's
in the pride of her young bearing, nor Katryn, not Gem

sitting in a corner of her pain, nor my aunt, the one
with the soft eyes that have soothed the one who writes this,

I would not break your heart, and you should know it;
I would not make you suffer, and you should know it;

and I am not suffering, but it is hard to know it.
I am wiser, I share the secret that is only a silence,

with the tyrants of the earth, with the man who piles rags
in a creaking cart, and goes around a corner

of a square at dusk. You measure my age wrongly,
I am not young now, nor old, not a child, nor a bud

snipped before it flowered, I am part of the muscle
of a galloping lion, or a bird keeping low over

dark canes; and what, in your sorrow, in our faces
howling like statues, you call a goodbye

is—I wish you would listen to me—a different welcome,
which you will share with me, and see that it is true.

All this the child spoke inside me, so I wrote it down.
As if his closing grave were the smile of the earth.

Sylvia Plath

The Colossus

I shall never get you put together entirely,
Pieced, glued, and properly jointed.
Mule-bray, pig-grunt and bawdy cackles
Proceed from your great lips.
It's worse than a barnyard.

Perhaps you consider yourself an oracle,
Mouthpiece of the dead, or of some god or other.
Thirty years now I have labored
To dredge the silt from your throat.
I am none the wiser.

Scaling little ladders with gluepots and pails of Lysol
I crawl like an ant in mourning
Over the weedy acres of your brow
To mend the immense skull-plates and clear
The bald, white tumuli of your eyes.

A blue sky out of the Oresteia
Arches above us. O father, all by yourself
You are pithy and historical as the Roman Forum.
I open my lunch on a hill of black cypress.
Your fluted bones and acanthine hair are littered

In their old anarchy to the horizon-line.
It would take more than a lightning-stroke
To create such a ruin.
Nights, I squat in the cornucopia
Of your left ear, out of the wind,

Counting the red stars and those of plum-color.
The sun rises under the pillar of your tongue.
My hours are married to shadow.
No longer do I listen for the scrape of a keel
On the blank stones of the landing.

Brendan Galvin

A Green Evening
September, 1952

I paused by the fence
and looked up,
and whatever happens
happened to make that sky
seem timeless,
awash with well-being,

as strongly delicate
as the odor an axe unlocks
from certain logs, that drifts
across the air as if
flowing from some deep-woods
bush in power.

I would have to go
as far into myself
as the archaeopteryx
is locked in Jurassic slate
to bring that evening back,
tied to it though I am.

I'd have to pick through
every filament,
brushing aside a dormouse
deep in a feeder
after sunflower seeds,
half-dollar size ears and all:
cedar shingles
curled to smiles on a roof:

even the rich cess of Drummer's Cove
at low tide,
and be able to erase
acres of asphalt slots
until scrub pine
reappeared, and the ancient clock
in an Esso station window,

to hold that central moment,
green and unbreakable, until
this fraying twist comes undone
and that evening
spreads everywhere, and I follow
the others over that fence
into the orchard again.

Charles Simic

Shirt

To get into it
As it lies
Crumpled on the floor
Without disturbing a single crease

Respectful
Of the way I threw it down
Last night
The way it happened to land

Almost managing
The impossible contortions
Doubling back now
Through a knotted sleeve

Michael S. Harper

The Families Album

Goggled mother with her children
stomp on the tar road,
their dresses black:
sugar maple, white pine,
apple tree, sumac,
young birch, red oak,
pine, cedar, deer moss
watch the archival print
in their death march,
for they lived here,
as they live with us now,
in these slanted pine floors
they tried to straighten,
in these squared windows
unsquared, in wallpaper torn
down, in the bare beams
of the addition plastered,
in a mother's covered eye
diseased by too much light,
too much blood which struck
her husband dead, too much
weed to make the farm work,
too many crooked doorways
on a dirt road tarred over.

This old house which was hers
made her crooked back a shingle,
her covered eye this fireplace oven,
her arms the young pine beams
now our clapboard siding;
the covered well runs in this dirt
basement, her spring watering her grave
where the fruit, vegetables, woodpile, lie.

Wesley McNair

The Minister's Death

That long fall,
when the voices stopped
in the tweed mouth
of his radio, and sermons
stood behind the door
of his study in files
no one would ever again inspect,
and even the black shoes
and vestments, emptied of him,
were closed away,
they sat together Sundays
in the house, now hers—
the son wearing his suit
and water-combed hair,
and mother in a housedress,
holding the dead
man's cane. Somewhere
at the edge of the new
feeling just beginning
between them, floorlamps
bloomed triple bulbs
and windowsills sagged
with African violets,
and the old woman,
not knowing exactly how
to say his face looked lovely
in the chair, encircled
by a white aura
of doily, said nothing
at all. And the son,
not used to feeling

small inside the great
shoulderpads of his suit,
looked down at the rugs
on rugs to where the trees kept
scattering the same, soft
puzzle of sunlight
until, from time to time,
she found the words
of an old dialogue they both
could speak: "How has the weather
been this week? What time
did you start out from Keene?"

Linda Gregg

To Be Here

The February road to the river is mud
and dirty snow, tire tracks and corncobs
uncovered by the mildness. I think I am
living alone and that I am not afraid.
Love is those birds working hard at flying
over the mountain going somewhere else.
Fidelity is always about what we have
already lived. I am happy, kicking snow.
The trees are the ones to honor. The trees
and the broken corn. And the clear sky
that looks like rain is falling through it.
Not a pretty spring, but the real thing.
The old weeds and the old vegetables.
Winter's graceful severity melting away.
I don't think the dead will speak.
I think they are happy just to be here.
If they did, I imagine them saying
birds flying, twigs, water reflecting.
There is only this. Dead weeds waiting
uncovered to the quiet soft day.

Louise Gluck

Field Flowers

What are you saying? That you want
eternal life? Are your thoughts really
as compelling as all that? Certainly
you don't look at us, don't listen to us,
on your skin
stain of sun, dust
of yellow buttercups: I'm talking
to you, you staring through
bars of high grass shaking
your little rattle— O
the soul! the soul! Is it enough
only to look inward? Contempt
for humanity is one thing, but why
disdain the expansive
field, your gaze rising over the clear heads
of the wild buttercups into what? Your poor
idea of heaven: absence
of change. Better than earth? How
would you know, who are neither
here nor there, standing in our midst?

Margaret Gibson

Beginner's Mind

When I begin to see
only what I've said—
my breath in the air
a snow of blind
keyholes and braille—
I let the dogs loose
in the field, and we run.
In the dimness of trees
by the wall, they chase
memories of squirrels.
I follow the wind until
out of breath
I crouch down in blank
snow, glad of the burn
of cold air in the west,
the border of trees
black and still.
Even now the magnolia
has buds, brushtips
of branches that lift
into the open.
Overhead, slate blue,
clouds swift along east.
I wait until stars
come into the blue—
then the black
never nowhere a child
gets quietly lost in.
I race the wind home.
In the kitchen new buds
of narcissus,

paperwhites unseasonal
in their bowl of stones
on the sill, have opened.
But my eye comes to rest
on a glass cup, cobalt blue,
which once, a child,
I named first when I named
what around me in the room
was living. I lift the glass,
turn it slowly in the light,
its whole body full of light.
Suddenly I hold everything
I know, myself most of all,
in question.

Jane Kenyon

Potato

In haste one evening while making dinner
I threw away a potato that was spoiled
on one end. The rest would have been

redeemable. In the yellow garbage pail
it became the consort of coffee grounds,
banana skins, carrot peelings.
I pitched it onto the compost
where steaming scraps and leaves
return, like bodies over time, to earth.

When I flipped the fetid layers with a hay
fork to air the pile, the potato turned up
unfailingly, as if to revile me—

looking plumper, firmer, resurrected
instead of disassembling. It seemed to grow
until I might have made shepherd's pie
for a whole hamlet, people who pass the day
dropping trees, pumping gas, pinning
hand-me-down clothes on the line.

Martín Espada

The Toolmaker Unemployed
Connecticut River Valley, 1992

The toolmaker
is sixty years old,
unemployed
since the letter
from his boss
at the machine shop.

He carries
a cooler of soda
everywhere,
so as not to carry
a flask of whiskey.

During the hours
of his shift,
he is building a barn
with borrowed lumber
or hacking at trees
in the yard.

The family watches
and listens to talk
of a bullet
in the forehead,
maybe for himself,
maybe for the man
holding the second mortgage.

Sometimes
he stares down
into his wallet.

III.

Fences

Here the poets turn more toward the relationship between the individual and society, a relation they see obstructed by massive difficulties, most of them reducible to the concept of walls. Frost makes a joke of the one he and his neighbor are mending, but seems to ask quite seriously if anything could be worse than the hollow truce it imposes. The latter, as the speaker of "Idiom of the Hero" sees it, is the state society has been in always, its economic classes hopelessly divided, its differences and inequities irresolvable. Like him, one may despair of such divisions and doubt the possibility of change; especially if one traverses any major city, as Stevens did on foot almost daily in Hartford. One may, like Warren in "Dream, Dump-Heap, and Civilization," feel a gnawing sense of guilt: the same sort of guilt that haunts Francis's poem "Blood Stains," written in response to the outward calm of Amherst during the war in Vietnam. Or one might, as in "For the Union Dead," stand appalled—by war, urban blight, and racism, all of which Robert Lowell sees emblemized in a fenced-off monument on Boston Common.

One gets a strong sense of wall from Meredith's "Effort at Speech," where an attempted mugging is to be seen as a violent effort to cross an economic barrier, a vast thickness of anger, shame, and fear, blocking any true communication between victim and attacker. They are both victims: of the same invisible wall that separates the two protagonists in Carruth's "The Mountain"; of the unmentioned assets from which the philanthropist, in Wilbur's "A Finished Man," sculpts his image of perfection; of the liquid profits that flow away from, and perpetuate, the little greeting card company in Dugan's "On Trading Time for Life by Work." Dugan, and especially Wilbur, are speaking of other things besides mammon. But surely money, or the lack of it, is a way of measuring the distance between the eternally good-for-nothing Scutz family and the proper upcountry citizenry represented by the speaker of "Saga." The Scutzes, however, know how to survive, possibly even thrive, and it may well be that Kumin's speaker feels a touch of envy.

The junk in the Scutzes' "yard" reappears in that of the broken-down family of McNair's "My Brother Running." It is what remains of their rural American dream of self-sufficiency, one they sought to realize in a failed nursery business long since conceded to Shop-Rite. Concentrated in the proverbial junk car, the dream, once an incentive, has become an economic roadblock that literally crushes the dreamer. Returning to poems of the city, we find another sort of "junk" buried in the language of Harper's "Makin' Jump Shots." In this graceful, seemingly lighthearted portrait of a youth practicing basketball on a neighborhood court, Harper has hidden some street jargon that refers to shooting not only baskets but heroin. The suggestion is that just outside the court (probably behind a steel fence) is a potential fate that threatens this picture, rendering the boy in his moment of glory extraordinarily fragile.

Walls, explicit in a few of the poems and implicit in most, restrict us from becoming a community in any true sense. Imposed from within and without, they result in mutual antagonism between individuals, classes, cultures. Between nations they result in belligerence—exemplified by the propaganda, arms production, and chauvinism confronted in Gibson's poem "Wars." History, there, is seen as "pain in movement," and even one's entry into the day is felt as a slow, painful motion against seemingly impossible odds. But sometimes, as in Espada's "Mi Vida," such walls are taken down, if only briefly. There a lawyer, unable to solve the eviction problems of a Guatemalan refugee, humbles himself before the suffering he witnesses. He can do nothing more—but his gesture, momentarily at least, dismantles the fences between his own socially accredited position and a person whom society totally excludes.

Robert Frost

Mending Wall

Something there is that doesn't love a wall,
That sends the frozen-ground-swell under it,
And spills the upper boulders in the sun;
And makes gaps even two can pass abreast.
The work of hunters is another thing:
I have come after them and made repair
Where they have left not one stone on a stone,
But they would have the rabbit out of hiding,
To please the yelping dogs. The gaps I mean,
No one has seen them made or heard them made,
But at spring mending-time we find them there.
I let my neighbor know beyond the hill;
And on a day we meet to walk the line
And set the wall between us once again.
We keep the wall between us as we go.
To each the boulders that have fallen to each.
And some are loaves and some so nearly balls
We have to use a spell to make them balance:
'Stay where you are until our backs are turned!'
We wear our fingers rough with handling them.
Oh, just another kind of outdoor game,
One on a side. It comes to little more:
There where it is we do not need the wall:
He is all pine and I am apple orchard.
My apple trees will never get across
And eat the cones under his pines, I tell him.
He only says, 'Good fences make good neighbors.'
Spring is the mischief in me, and I wonder
If I could put a notion in his head:
'*Why* do they make good neighbors? Isn't it
Where there are cows? But here there are no cows.

Before I built a wall I'd ask to know
What I was walling in or walling out,
And to whom I was like to give offense.
Something there is that doesn't love a wall,
That wants it down.' I could say 'Elves' to him,
But it's not elves exactly, and I'd rather
He said it for himself. I see him there
Bringing a stone grasped firmly by the top
In each hand, like an old-stone savage armed.
He moves in darkness as it seems to me,
Not of woods only and the shade of trees.
He will not go behind his father's saying,
And he likes having thought of it so well
He says again, 'Good fences make good neighbors.'

Wallace Stevens

Idiom of the Hero

I heard two workers say, "This chaos
Will soon be ended."

This chaos will not be ended,
The red and the blue house blended,

The man that is poor at night
Attended

Like the man that is rich and right.
The great men will not be blended . . .

I am the poorest of all.
I know that I cannot be mended,

Out of the clouds, pomp of the air,
By which at least I am befriended.

Archibald MacLeish

Long Hot Summer

Never again
when the heat overwhelms us
cool elms.

The elm leaves shrivel on the twig
and the sun beats through and our time is big
with a lidless time that knows no dark,
no shadow where the heart can see,
no shade at noon where doubt can be.

The beetle of God is under the bark
and the age of the leafy trees is done:
the cities are dying one by one
of the heat and the hate and the naked sun.

Never again
when the hate overwhelms us
cool elms.

Robert Francis

Blood Stains

blood stains   how to remove   from cotton
silk   from all fine fabrics   blood stains
where did I read   all I remember old stains
harder than fresh   old stains often indelible

blood stains   what did it say   from glass
shattered   from metal   memorial marble
how to remove   a clean soft cloth   was it
and plenty of tepid water   also from paper

headlines   dispatches   communiqués   history
white leaves   green leaves   from grass growing
or dead   from trees   from flowers   from sky
from standing from running water   blood stains

Richard Eberhart

Spite Fence

After years of bickerings

Family one
Put up a spite fence
Against family two.

Cheek by cheek
They couldn't stand it.
The Maine village

Looked so peaceful.
We drove through yearly,
We didn't know.

Now if you drive through
You see the split wood,
Thin and shrill.

But who's who?
Who made it,
One side or the other?

Bad neighbors make good fencers.

Robert Penn Warren

Dream, Dump-Heap, and Civilization

Like the stench and smudge of the old dump-heap
Of Norwalk, Connecticut, the residue

Of my dream remains, but I make no
Sense of even the fragments. They are nothing

More significant than busted iceboxes and stinking mattresses
Of Norwalk, and other such human trash from which

Smudge rose by day, or coals winked red by night,
Like a sign to the desert-walkers

Blessed by God's promise. Keep your foot on the gas,
And you'll get to Westport. But

What of my dream—stench, smudge, and fragments?
And behind it all a morning shadow, like guilt, strives.

To say what? How once I had lied to my mother and hid
In a closet and said, in darkness, aloud: "I hate you"?

Or how once, in total fascination, I watched a black boy
Take a corn knife and decapitate six kittens? Did I dream

That again last night? How he said: "Too many, dem"?
Did I dream of six kitten-heads staring all night at me?

All try to say something—still now trying
By daylight? Their blood inexhaustibly drips. Did I wake

With guilt? How rarely is air here pure as in the Montana mountains!
Sometime we must probe more deeply the problem of complicity.

Is civilization possible without it?

Stanley Kunitz

Robin Redbreast

It was the dingiest bird
you ever saw, all the color
washed from him, as if
he had been standing in the rain,
friendless and stiff and cold,
since Eden went wrong.
In the house marked For Sale,
where nobody made a sound,
in the room where I lived
with an empty page, I had heard
the squawking of the jays
under the wild persimmons
tormenting him.
So I scooped him up
after they knocked him down,
in league with that ounce of heart
pounding in my palm,
that dumb beak gaping.
Poor thing! Poor foolish life!
without sense enough to stop
running in desperate circles,
needing my lucky help
to toss him back into his element.
But when I held him high,
fear clutched my hand,
for through the hole in his head,
cut whistle-clean . . .

through the old dried wound
between his eyes
where the hunter's brand
had tunneled out his wits . . .
I caught the cold flash of the blue
unappeasable sky.

Constance Carrier

Pro Patria

On a green island in the Main Street traffic
is a granite arch to the dead of the Civil War—
in the Eastlake style, all cubes and tetrahedrons,
each end of the passage barred by an iron-lace door.

They are always locked, tho the space between is empty—
from door to door it isn't much over a yard:
break open one, you could almost touch the other.
Nobody knows what the locks were meant to guard.

East and west, the head of a blank-eyed lion
hisses an arc of spray to the pool below
with a faint persistent sound, an endless whisper
steady under the traffic's stop-and-go.

On top of the monument stands a gilded lady
casting a wreath forever into space:
her carven robes are decent and concealing:
there is no emotion graven on her face.

Words are cut in the stone above the arches—
THEY JOINED THE MORTAL STRUGGLE AND WENT DOWN
and on every quoin is written the name of a battle
that bloodied creek or landing, bluff or town

now dry and hard in history and granite . . .
In summer the sun lies hot upon the stone,
and the bums and the drunks and the old men and the pigeons
take over the little island for their own.

The old men sit on a bench, with nuts and breadcrusts
for the birds to eat from their hands: the ne'er-do-wells
sprawl on the grass and drowse and boast and argue:
the drunks discourse like statesmen and oracles,

while the birds skim over their heads with a cardboard clatter
of wings, or mince on the pavement at their feet . . .
They are all of them tolerant of one another
in this world like a bubble, this island in the street.

The sun is warm, the lions hiss, and the faithful
loaf in their places, lazy and benign,
a little hierarchy who inherit
this plot of earth, this obsolescent shrine.

Who can recall the day of that war's ending?
Think of our own time, then, the summer night
when the word came, and all the churchbells sounded
the end of the dark and the coming of the light.

How many times how many towns have seen it,
the light, the hope, the promise, after the dark—
seen it, and watched it flicker and ebb and vanish,
leaving no trace except some little park

where no one recalls that dream, that disillusion,
and a monument to death is only known
as a place where the harmless unambitious gather
and the doves come down for bread on the sun-warmed stone.

Elizabeth Bishop

Varick Street

> At night the factories
> struggle awake,
> wretched uneasy buildings
> veined with pipes
> attempt their work.
> Trying to breathe,
> the elongated nostrils
> haired with spikes
> give off such stenches, too.

And I shall sell you sell you
sell you of course, my dear, and you'll sell me.

> On certain floors
> certain wonders.
> Pale dirty light,
> some captured iceberg
> being prevented from melting.
> See the mechanical moons,
> sick, being made
> to wax and wane
> at somebody's instigation.

And I shall sell you sell you
sell you of course, my dear, and you'll sell me.

> Lights music of love
> work on. The presses
> print calendars

I suppose; the moons
make medicine
or confectionery. Our bed
shrinks from the soot
and hapless odors
hold us close.

And I shall sell you sell you
sell you of course, my dear, and you'll sell me.

Robert Lowell

For the Union Dead

"Relinquunt Omnia Servare Rem Publicam."

The old South Boston Aquarium stands
in a Sahara of snow now. Its broken windows are boarded.
The bronze weathervane cod has lost half its scales.
The airy tanks are dry.

Once my nose crawled like a snail on the glass;
my hand tingled
to burst the bubbles
drifting from the noses of the cowed, compliant fish.

My hand draws back. I often sigh still
for the dark downward and vegetating kingdom
of the fish and reptile. One morning last March,
I pressed against the new barbed and galvanized

fence on the Boston Common. Behind their cage,
yellow dinosaur steamshovels were grunting
as they cropped up tons of mush and grass
to gouge their underworld garage.

Parking spaces luxuriate like civic
sandpiles in the heart of Boston.
A girdle of orange, Puritan-pumpkin colored girders
braces the tingling Statehouse,

shaking over the excavations, as it faces Colonel Shaw
and his bell-cheeked Negro infantry
on St. Gaudens' shaking Civil War relief,
propped by a plank splint against the garage's earthquake.

Two months after marching through Boston,
half the regiment was dead;
at the dedication,
William James could almost hear the bronze Negroes breathe.

Their monument sticks like a fishbone
in the city's throat.
Its Colonel is as lean
as a compass-needle.

He has an angry wrenlike vigilance,
a greyhound's gentle tautness;
he seems to wince at pleasure,
and suffocate for privacy.

He is out of bounds now. He rejoices in man's lovely,
peculiar power to choose life and die—
when he leads his black soldiers to death,
he cannot bend his back.

On a thousand small town New England greens,
the old white churches hold their air
of sparse, sincere rebellion; frayed flags
quilt the graveyards of the Grand Army of the Republic.

The stone statues of the abstract Union Soldier
grow slimmer and younger each year—
wasp-waisted, they doze over muskets
and muse through their sideburns . . .

Shaw's father wanted no monument
except the ditch,
where his son's body was thrown
and lost with his "niggers."

The ditch is nearer.
There are no statues for the last war here;
on Boylston Street, a commercial photograph
shows Hiroshima boiling

over a Mosler Safe, the "Rock of Ages"
that survived the blast. Space is nearer.
When I crouch to my television set,
the drained faces of Negro school-children rise like balloons.

Colonel Shaw
is riding on his bubble,
he waits
for the blessèd break.

The Aquarium is gone. Everywhere,
giant finned cars nose forward like fish;
a savage servility
slides by on grease.

William Meredith

Effort at Speech
for Muriel Rukeyser

Climbing the stairway grey with urban midnight,
Cheerful, venial, ruminating pleasure,
Darkness takes me, an arm around my throat and
                    Give me your wallet.

Fearing cowardice more than other terrors,
Angry I wrestle with my unseen partner,
Caught in a ritual not of our own making,
                    panting like spaniels.

Bold with adrenalin, mindless, shaking,
God damn it, no! I rasp at him behind me,
Wrenching the leather wallet from his grasp. It
                    breaks like a wishbone,

So that departing (routed by my shouting,
Not by my strength or inadvertent courage)
Half of the papers lending me a name are
                    gone with him nameless.

Only now turning, I see a tall boy running,
Fifteen, sixteen, dressed thinly for the weather.
Reaching the streetlight he turns a brown face briefly
                    phrased like a question.

I like a questioner watch him turn the corner
Taking the answer with him, or his half of it.
Loneliness, not a sensible emotion,
                    breathes hard on the stairway.

Walking homeward I fraternize with shadows,
Zig-zagging with them where they flee the streetlights,
Asking for trouble, asking for the message
                    trouble had sent me.

All fall down has been scribbled on the street in
Garbage and excrement: so much for the vision
Others taunt me with, my untimely humor,
                    so much for cheerfulness.

Next time don't wrangle, give the boy the money,
Call across chasms what the world you know is.
Luckless and lied to, how can a child master
                    human decorum?

Next time a switch-blade, somewhere he is thinking,
I should have killed him and took the lousy wallet.
Reading my cards he feels a surge of anger
                    blind as my shame.

Error from Babel mutters in the places,
Cities apart, where now we word our failures:
Hatred and guilt have left us without language
                    who might have held discourse.

Hayden Carruth

The Mountain

Black summer, black Vermont. Who sees
this mountain rising nearby
in the darkness? But we

know it there. On the other side
in a black street of a black city
a man who is probably black

carries a Thompson
submachinegun, and don't
tell me how that feels

who carried one two years
in Italy; blunt-barreled power,
smooth simple unfailing mechanism

—the only gun whose recoil
tugs you forward, toward
the target, almost

like love. Separated
by this immense hill we share nevertheless
a certain knowledge of tactics

and a common attitude toward reality.
Flickering neon, like moonlight in beech leaves,
is fine camouflage. To destroy

can be beautiful.
I remember Mussolini's
bombed statues by the *dopolavoro* pavilion,

thick monsters transformed to elegance
by their broken heads and cut-off
arms. Let the city be transformed.

A man with a submachinegun is
invulnerable, the sniper's
sharp little steel or the fist

of a grenade always
finds him surprised. Hey,
look out, man! What you

trying to do, get yourself
killed? They're everywhere, everywhere,
hear? —the night's

full of them and they're looking
for a dead nigger—so watch it,
and go on fox feet and listen like a bat;

remember everything I told you.
You got to be smart enough
for both of us now.

But are you there? Are you
really there?

Richard Wilbur

A Finished Man

Of the four louts who threw him off the dock
Three are now dead, and so more faintly mock
The way he choked and splashed and was afraid.
His memory of the fourth begins to fade.

It was himself whom he could not forgive;
Yet it has been a comfort to outlive
That woman, stunned by his appalling gaffe,
Who with a napkin half-suppressed her laugh,

Or that grey colleague, surely gone by now,
Who, turning toward the window, raised his brow,
Embarrassed to have caught him in a lie.
All witness darkens, eye by dimming eye.

Thus he can walk today with heart at ease
Through the old quad, escorted by trustees,
To dedicate the monumental gym
A grateful college means to name for him.

Seated, he feels the warm sun sculpt his cheek
As the young president gets up to speak.
If the dead die, if he can but forget,
If money talks, he may be perfect yet.

Alan Dugan

On Trading Time for Life by Work

The receptionist has shiny fingernails
since she has buffed them up for hours,
not for profit but for art, while they,
the partners, have been arguing themselves
the further into ruthless paranoia,
the accountant said. The sales representatives
came out against the mustard yellow: "It
looks like baby-shit," and won, as ever. In
the studio, the artist, art director, and
the copy chief were wondering out loud:
Whether a "Peace On Earth" or a "Love
And Peace On Earth" should go around
the trumpeting angel on the Christmas card.
In this way the greeting card company
worked back and forth across a first spring
afternoon like a ferryboat on the river:
time was passing, it itself was staying the same,
and workers rode it on the running depths
while going nowhere back and forth across
the surface of the river. Profits flow away
in this game, and thank god there is none
of the transcendence printed on the product.

Maxine Kumin

Saga

1. Life Style

Invincible begetters, assorted Scutzes
have always lived hereabouts in the woods
trapping beaver or fox, poaching enough
deer to get by on. Winters, they barricade
their groundsills with spoiled hay, which can ignite
from a careless cigarette or chimney spark.
In the fifties, one family barely got out
when the place lit up like the Fair midway at dark.

The singular name of Scutz, it is thought, derives
from *skuft,* Middle Dutch for the nape one is strung up by.
Hangmen or hanged, they led the same snug lives
in an Old World loft adjoining the pigsty
as now, three generations tucked in two
rooms with color tv, in the New.

2. Leisure

The seldom-traveled dirt road by their door
is where, good days, the Scutzes take their ease.
It serves as living room, garage, *pissoir*
as well as barnyard. Hens scratch and rabbits doze
under cars jacked up on stumps of trees.

Someone produces a dozen bottles of beer.
Someone tacks a target to a tire
across the road and hoists it seductively
human-high. The Scutzes love to shoot.
Later, they line the empty bottles up.

The music of glassbreak gladdens them. The brute
sound of a bullet widening a rip
in rubber, the rifle kick, the powder smell
pure bliss. Deadeyes, the Scutzes lightly kill.

3. Shelter

Old doors slanted over packing crates
shelter the Scutzes' several frantic dogs
pinioned on six-foot chains they haven't been
loosed from since January of '91
when someone on skis crept up in snow fog
and undid all of their catches in the night.

Each of the Scutzes' dogs has a dish or plate
to eat from, usually overturned in the dirt.
What do they do for water? Pray for rain.
What do they do for warmth? Remember when
they lay in the litter together, a sweet
jumble of laundry, spotted and stained.

O we are smug in the face of the Scutzes, we
who stroll past their domain, its aromas of ripe decay,
its casual discards mottled with smut and pee.
What do we neighbors do? Look the other way.

4. Self-fulfilling Prophecy

If Lonnie Scutz comes back, he's guaranteed
free room and board in the State's crowbar hotel.
His girlfriend Grace, a toddler at her heels
and in her arms a grubby ten-month jewel,
looks to be pregnant again, but not his seed.
It's rumored this one was sired by his dad.

Towheads with skyblue eyes, they'll go to school
now and then, struggle to learn to read
and write, forget to carry when they add,
be mocked, kept back or made to play the fool
and soon enough drop out. Their nimble code,
hit first or get hit, supplants the Golden Rule.

It all works out the way we knew it would.
They'll come to no good end, the Scutzes' kids.

Philip Booth

Game

Between periods,

                boys at the urinals,
boymen, menboys, telling AIDS jokes,
yelling *Ain't the game great.*

                           Jesus,
'djou see 'em rack that one up
right at the goal . . .

                      Freshman girls
in the stands,

                screaming at referees
their fathers' utmost obscenities.
They must have learned

                    in the womb,
here or in Rome, at some earlier series,
limp but awake, the way,

                    in their parents' arms,
tonight's kids are fallen.

                  The other side
of the glass partition

                the hurt players lie,
scattered like death at Antietam,
the trainers working over them, working
them over,

              to get them back in the game.
O, its sheer violence,

                our innate violence,

my anger squared in that tight arena
until I could not speak, or stay, but
walked myself out into winter sky,

                                    out through
a door where a woman stamped me
with an ink pinetree,

                        sure,
since I'd paid so much,
I would come back in.

Galway Kinnell

The Tragedy of Bricks

1

The twelve-noon whistle groans
its puff of steam high up on the smokestack.
Out of the brickwork the lace-workers
come carrying empty black lunch-stomachs.
The noontime composition consists
of that one blurry bass note
in concert with the tenor of the stomachs.
The used-up lace-worker bicycling past,
who is about a hundred, suctions together mouth-matter,
tongue-hurls it at the gate of the mill, rattles away.
A spot of gold rowels its trajectory
of contempt across a boy's memory.

2

Overhead the sea blows upside down across Rhode Island.
slub clump slub clump
Charlie drops out. Carl steps in.
slub clump
No hitch in the sequence.
Paddy stands down. Otto jumps up.
They say Otto in his lifetime clumped into place seven million
    bricks,
then fell from the scaffolding,
clump.
slub clump slub clump
Jake takes over from Otto, slubs mortar onto brick, clumps brick
    onto mortar.
Does this. Does it again. Wears out.
Topples over. No pause.
Rene appears. Homer collapses. Angelo springs up. No break in the
    rhythm.

slub clump slub clump
They wear in they wear out.
They lay the bricks that build the mills
that shock the Blackstone River into yellow froth.

3

Here come the joggers.
I am sixty-one. The joggers are approximately very young.
They run for fun through a world where everyone used to lay bricks
    for work.
Their faces tell there is a hell and they will reach it.

4

Fall turns into winter,
poplars stand with their pants down.
The five o'clock whistle blurts.
The lace-workers straggle out again
from under the tragedy of bricks.
Some trudge off,
others sit between disks
of piano wire and wobble into the dusk.

5

A bricklayer walks the roof of the mill.
He carries a lantern, like a father,
which has a tongue in it, which does not speak, like a father.
He is there to make sure no brick fails in its duty.
A boy born among the bricks walks
on packed snow under the walls of the mill.
Under each step the snow sounds
the small crushed shrieks
of all the bricklayers, who lie stacked
somewhere hereabout. Suddenly the full moon
lays out across the imperfect world
everything's grave.
From the mill

comes slub clump slub clump. The boy knows
his father and mother will disappear
before the least brick cracks or tells its story,
an antecedence once known as infernal corrosion.
When the boy grows up it will have laid the footing for the concept
    of the neutron bomb.
Which eats first the living forms,
and after that the windows and doors.

Anne Sexton

Mr. Mine

Notice how he has numbered the blue veins
in my breast. Moreover there are ten freckles.
Now he goes left. Now he goes right.
He is building a city, a city of flesh.
He's an industrialist. He has starved in cellars
and, ladies and gentlemen, he's been broken by iron,
by the blood, by the metal, by the triumphant
iron of his mother's death. But he begins again.
Now he constructs me. He is consumed by the city.
From the glory of boards he has built me up.
From the wonder of concrete he has molded me.
He has given me six hundred street signs.
The time I was dancing he built a museum.
He built ten blocks when I moved on the bed.
He constructed an overpass when I left.
I gave him flowers and he built an airport.
For traffic lights he handed out red and green
lollipops. Yet in my heart I am go children slow.

Donald Hall

from *The One Day*

There are ways to get rich: Find an old corporation,
self-insured, with capital reserves. Borrow
to buy: Then dehire managers; yellow-slip maintenance;
pay public relations to explain how winter is summer;
liquidate reserves and distribute cash in dividends:
Get out, sell stock for capital gains, reward the usurer,
and look for new plunder—leaving a milltown devastated,
workers idle on streetcorners, broken equipment, no cash
for repair or replacement, no inventory or credit.
Then vote for the candidate who abolishes foodstamps.

—

Or: Buy fifty acres of pasture from the widower:
Survey, cut a road, subdivide; bulldoze the unpainted
barn, selling eighteenth-century beams with bark
still on them; bulldoze foundation granite that oxen sledded;
bulldoze stone walls set with lost skill; bulldoze the Cape
the widower lived in; bulldoze his father's seven-apple tree.
Drag the trailer from the scraggly orchard to the dump:
Let the poor move into the spareroom of their town
cousins; pave garden and cornfield; build weekend houses
for skiers and swimmers; build Slope 'n' Shore; name the new

road Blueberry Muffin Lane; build Hideaway Homes
for executives retired from pricefixing for General Electric
and migrated north out of Greenwich to play bridge
with neighbors migrated north out of Darien. Build huge

centrally heated Colonial ranches—brick, stone, and wood
confounded together—on pasture slopes that were white
with clover, to block public view of Blue Mountain.
Invest in the firm foreclosing Kansas that exchanges
topsoil for soybeans. Vote for a developer as United States
senator. Vote for statutes that outlaw visible poverty.

John Hollander

A Late Fourth

Firecrackers sounding like shots of handguns rattle
The afternoon of early July at a late time
For celebrations and it is an inglorious
Fourth we have come to, like the birthday of a very
Sick man: no simple affirmations will do today.
In the dying wind the nation's stars and stripes slacken;
I guess this must be the flag of its disposition
Not to save itself. Only now, much later, all flags
Down for the night, we watch some bunting—no more a flag
Than the flag is our old glory—as it fitfully
Gleams in the streetlamp's conditional light, like a truth
Which the sad, difficult telling of half-conceals, half-
Discloses, through our few tears ungleaming in the dark.

Derek Walcott

Midsummer: XXX

Gold dung and urinous straw from the horse garages,
click-clop of hooves sparking cold cobblestone.
From bricked-in carriage yards, exhaling arches
send the stale air of transcendental Boston—
tasselled black hansoms trotting under elms,
tilting their crops to the shade of Henry James.
I return to the city of my exile down Storrow Drive,
the tunnel with its split seraphs flying *en face,*
with finite sorrow; blocks long as paragraphs
pass in a style to which I'm not accustomed,
since, if I were, I would have been costumed
to drape the cloaks of couples who arrive
for dinner, drawing their chairs from tables where each glass,
catching the transcendental clustered lights,
twirled with perceptions. Style is character—
so my forehead crusts like brick, my sockets char
like a burnt brownstone in the Negro Quarter;
but when a fog obscures the Boston Common
and, up Beacon Hill, the old gas standards stutter
to save their period, I see a black coachman,
with gloves as white as his white-ankled horse,
who counts their laughter, their lamplit good nights,
then jerks the reins of his brass-handled hearse.

Sylvia Plath

Night Shift

It was not a heart, beating,
That muted boom, that clangor
Far off, not blood in the ears
Drumming up any fever

To impose on the evening.
The noise came from outside:
A metal detonating
Native, evidently, to

These stilled suburbs: nobody
Startled at it, though the sound
Shook the ground with its pounding.
It took root at my coming

Till the thudding source, exposed,
Confounded inept guesswork:
Framed in windows of Main Street's
Silver factory, immense

Hammers hoisted, wheels turning,
Stalled, let fall their vertical
Tonnage of metal and wood;
Stunned the marrow. Men in white

Undershirts circled, tending
Without stop those greased machines,
Tending, without stop, the blunt
Indefatigable fact.

Brendan Galvin

A Photo of Miners
USA, 1908

With trees backing them
instead of the pit's mouth,
they could have been
at a fifth grade picnic.
But the spit-baller won't grow into
his father's jacket, and a ladder
of safety pins climbs the front of
the class clown. Stretch,
who got tall the soonest,
has the air of a chimney sweep,
and here is a little grandfather
in brogans and rag gloves,
his face shoved between two shoulders
his arms are draping,
his eyes flashing the riding lights
of pain. They are a year's
supply, average age, give or take
a year: ten. Don't look for
a bare foot at a devil-may-care
angle on one of the rails,
or a habitable face for a life
you might have led—that
mouth is rigid as a mailslot,
the light on those hands predicts
common graves. Does anything transcend
the wall-eyed patience of beasts,
the artless smirk on the boy
with the high forehead
who thinks he will croon his way
out of this?

Charles Simic

Grocery

Figure or figures unknown
Keep a store
Keep it open
Nights and all day Sunday

Half of what they sell
Will kill you
The other half
Makes you go back for more

Too cheap to turn on the lights
Hard to tell what it is
They've got on the counter
What it is you're paying for

All the rigors
All the solemnities
Of a brass scale imperceptibly quivering
In the early winter dusk

One of its pans
For their innards
The other one for yours—
And yours heavier

Michael S. Harper

Makin' Jump Shots

He waltzes into the lane
'cross the free-throw line,
fakes a drive, pivots,
floats from the asphalt turf
in an arc of black light,
and sinks two into the chains.

One on one he fakes
down the main, passes
into the free lane
and hits the chains.

A sniff in the fallen air—
he stuffs it through the chains
riding high:
"traveling" someone calls—
and he laughs, stepping
to a silent beat, gliding
as he sinks two into the chains.

Wesley McNair

My Brother Running: V

When my stepfather died in the summer
of 1985, everybody in the whole country
seemed to be at the movies, watching the second term
of Ronald Reagan, who'd just come to town in a blur
of flags, won the nation's heart and was romancing her
in the longest feature he'd ever made. Big business
was up, defense spending was up, Christa McAuliffe
was in Washington promising to take the souls
of everyone who hadn't won the Teachernaut contest up

with her. That summer in New Hampshire, meanwhile,
my stepfather got down under the same junk car
he'd owned all his life, pulled out the transmission,
and in what must have been a mixture of surprise
and recognition, watched the thing roll off
its blocks on top of him and snuff
his asthmatic breath. It hits me now
that nobody was there, any more than we were there
when my brother, shortly afterward, sat in the darkness

with the woman in his head, bent over his Nikes.
The radio in the grass beside the collapsed car
whispered a golden oldie to itself.
In the barn behind it, broken hoes
and wrong-side-up spades stood there
looking at nothing, and far off where plants
broke out of their pots and vetch twined,
the rows of twenty-five years' worth
of a failed nursery went on falling

out of perspective, collecting the dark—
the whole weedy empire lost
to the Shop-Rite bush and tree concession
off I-89, and he himself now lost
with it: the father of his stepsons' trauma,
the father of Working To Earn the Joy
That Never Comes. No more anger
about the life which, hands full right
to the end, he could not grasp and take;

no more in those dead ears the voice
of his wife saying, you always, you never,
the voice become his own; only
the wild, repetitious stuttering of goats
unmilked and unfed in their pen
until I myself arrived to milk and feed them,
and my brother came, and the three of us,
all that could be salvaged from the dead
habit of family, went together into that dark,

my mother in the lead saying, What
is going to happen to me next,
Bob close behind with the flashlight asking
How could he have *owned* such a car, and I,
unable to take in how old my mother seemed,
how fat my brother had got and the death
all at the same time. Then my brother touched
the light on the old junker, deep in its tires.
Then he touched it on the matted grass

and while my mother, too bitter and tired almost
to care, told how Lloyd come over
to jack the damn thing up and pull the body out,
I saw the image of my stepfather's face,
free of its cap and floating in its hair,
eyes closed against the world of auto parts
and all the other pieces he could not
find a way to fit together, this world
which he now left to each of us.

Linda Gregg

The Shopping-Bag Lady

You told people I would know easily what the murdered
lady had in her sack which could prove she was happy
more or less. As if they were a game, the old women
who carry all they own in bags, maybe proudly,
without homes we think except the streets.
But if I could guess (nothing in sets for example),
I would not. They are like those men who lay their
few things on the ground in a park at the end of Hester.
For sale perhaps, but who can tell? Like her way
of getting money. Never asking. Sideways and disconcerting.
With no thanks, only judgment. "You are a nice girl,"
one said as she moved away and then stopped in front
of a bum sitting on the bench who yelled that he would
kill her if she did not get away from him. She walked
at an angle not exactly away but until she was the same
distance from each of us. Stood still, looking down.
Standing in our attention as if it were a palpable thing.
Like the city itself or the cold winter. Holding her hands.
And if there was disgrace, it was God's. The failure
was ours as she remained quiet near the concrete wall
with cars coming and the sound of the subway filling
and fading in the most important place we have yet devised.

Louise Gluck

Daisies

Go ahead: say what you're thinking. The garden
is not the real world. Machines
are the real world. Say frankly what any fool
could read in your face: it makes sense
to avoid us, to resist
nostalgia. It is
not modern enough, the sound the wind makes
stirring a meadow of daisies: the mind
cannot shine following it. And the mind
wants to shine, plainly, as
machines shine, and not
grow deep, as, for example, roots. It is very touching,
all the same, to see you cautiously
approaching the meadow's border in early morning,
when no one could possibly
be watching you. The longer you stand at the edge,
the more nervous you seem. No one wants to hear
impressions of the natural world: you will be
laughed at again; scorn will be piled on you.
As for what you're actually
hearing this morning: think twice
before you tell anyone what was said in this field
and by whom.

Margaret Gibson

Wars

1. Documentary

Men in stout uniforms, helmets like tortoise
shells, glide on parquet,
brush past a carved mantel, rococo and cool.
Empires fall, a voice tells us, slowly.
The rain falls and in it blossoms of smoke
profoundly cease fire.

The narrator, if you believe his voice, tells
history as if it were a thing of the past,
but his voice travels out into waves
of dark galaxies light years away,
the word *war*

grandly pronounced, wonderful as any
Sapphic poem or Persian
shard.

2. An Ordinary Moment Between Wars

It's noon. The whistle blows in air like fetid
fruit. The factories simmer.

As I sit here wondering what to make
of an English veteran I've remembered—
brought to the theatre in a basket,
arms cut off to the collarbone,
legs sheared to the crotch,
compact and speaking of Oscar Wilde,
"All art is useless"—

as I sit here, the workers from Electric Boat
make their run through the company
gates for liquor.

3. Civilians

When my uncle speaks of war,
dignity buttons on him like a linen vest.
Only the Germans were cruel.
When he ridicules Asian peasants,
his feet do a tap dance in their good
leather and brown polished wingtips.

I keep wanting to see them under a chest
of bamboo in Da Nang, in a bedroom
whose walls fly out in one blast
leaving the floor like a tea tray,
one wrought iron railing in place,
the chest, and those terrible
empty shoes.

4. Cold Wars Inside

Asleep
I cross over rivers into a dream, carried by pain
in a gaunt man's face. He reads me ancient
documents. Centuries crack. Old conquerors
leave the left-alive beseeching the moon,
their hands cut off, flung at their feet
like forgotten gloves.

Now morning
snow falls like sand in an hourglass
close-up. History is pain in movement,
Burkhardt said. It was his face in the dream.
My feet touch the cold floor. I move into a day
that opens like any other in history, grand and numb.

Jane Kenyon

Back from the City

After three days and nights of rich food
and late talk in overheated rooms,
of walks between mounds of garbage
and human forms bedded down for the night
under rags, I come back to my dooryard,
to my own wooden step.

The last red leaves fall to the ground
and frost has blackened the herbs and asters
that grew beside the porch. The air
is still and cool, and the withered grass
lies flat in the field. A nuthatch spirals
down the rough trunk of the tree.

At the Cloisters I indulged in piety
while gazing at a painted lindenwood Pietà—
Mary holding her pierced and desiccated son
across her knees; but when a man stepped close
under the tasseled awning of the hotel,
asking for "a quarter for someone
down on his luck," I quickly turned my back.

Now I hear tiny bits of bark and moss
break off under the bird's beak and claw,
and fall onto already-fallen leaves.
"Do you love me?" said Christ to his disciple.
"Lord, you know
that I love you."
                    "Then feed my sheep."

Martín Espada

Mi Vida: Wings of Fright
Chelsea, Massachusetts, 1987

The refugee's run
across the desert borderlands
carved wings of fright
into his forehead,
growing more crooked
with every eviction notice
in this waterfront city of the north.

He sat in the office for the poor,
daughter burrowed asleep
on one shoulder,
and spoke to the lawyer
with a voice trained obedient
in the darkness of church confessionals
and police barracks, Guatemalan dusk.

The lawyer nodded through papers,
glancing up only when the girl awoke
to spout white vomit on the floor
and her father's shirt.
"Mi vida": My life, he said,
then said again, as he bundled her
to the toilet.

This was how the lawyer,
who, like the fortune-teller,
had a bookshelf of prophecy
but a cabinet empty of cures,
found himself
kneeling on the floor
with a paper towel.

IV.

The Road There

Poems can offer no cures. But they can diagnose, as we have seen, and they can prophesy a healing by pointing the way. Sometimes one may have to distance oneself to get there. Frost's "Birches" does so by moving momentarily heavenward, to clear a world-weary mind, then coming back to earth, "the right place for love." Not dissimilarly, Stevens's "Martial Cadenza" looks to the silent indifference of the evening star for an ultimate contradiction to evils such as the holocaust, warfare, and the armaments momentarily seen "fixed fast in a profound defeat." The sense of timeless calm expressed by Stevens is not far removed from the "old strange personal unconcern" experienced by Carruth as he reflects, under falling snow, on the relative inconsequence of his own mortality.

Though they briefly take a distance, these poems are not evasive. By opening the mind to something far greater than itself, their contemplation of the universe can provide us with a proper sense of humility. Against that "vastly superior page"—to quote Plath—our selves, our thoughts, even our very words, may seem small indeed; but the view does not demean us. On the contrary, it can bring us to the realization that infinity is not just overhead but in all things here: we need only drop our gaze to what Lowell calls "the true and insignificant"—a pebble, a leaf, a chip of wood—and discover ourselves there before our eyes move on.

Perhaps the sense of such connectedness is what a child in the twilit evening is dancing to, in the lightfooted rhythm of MacLeish's "Where the Hayfields Were;" and what a mower and his horses are moving to, in the slow turning of Francis's "The Sound I Listened For." The relation of the girl to the air, of the mower to the horses, is reciprocal: like that of Eberhart to a squirrel, Warren to a cloud, Kunitz to a pair of snakes, and Kinnell (as St. Francis) to a sow. They are conjoined, each to each, by touch, sight, thought, motion, or sound—just as Carrier is reassimilated, by a familiar voice, into the town from which she has been physically and mentally estranged. Even the crowds and classes of a city are momentarily integrated, in Bishop's "Anaphora," by the sun which falls upon their faces with the light of continuous affirmation, and hope.

Judicious hope, hope tempered by mindfulness, resonates in Meredith's "The Cheer" and in Wilbur's "Advice to a Prophet," each of which replies in its own way to the trumpeters of doomsday. Hope comes disguised with irony in "Thesis, Antithesis, and Nostalgia," Dugan's bittersweet reflection on perpetuity, then appears more humorously in Kumin's "The Excrement Poem," the substance of whose title unites all creatures in a venerable, ongoing industry. Hope is expressed more seriously again by Booth's "Presence," where the very existence of human and animal life is seen as an undeniable wonder. Not to be kept from the latter are the lives of plants and even stones, which Hall's "Granite and Grass" perceives as essentially the same, and, within the continuum of time, inseparable from ours. Stones, in Hollander's "One of Our Walks," form the inescapable bed in which the brookwater of the living present flows.

In Walcott's "The Season of Phantasmal Peace," continuance, hope, and kinship with other beings are interwoven in one long moment of healing. The healers are hosts of migrating birds flying over country and city, and the healing is the lifting from us of a shadow. In place of it the birds cast over us light that cannot be seen. This is the same invisible light that passes unstated between two lovers, at the end of Sexton's "I Remember." In Simic's "Spring" it is the laughter of a woman pinning up her laundry. In Harper's poem it is an apple tree whose roots are the intertwining histories of races. It is what Galvin's blue heron stands for, and what McNair's townspeople hold in their hands, and in Gluck's poem it is a flower opening. It is the simple exchange of speech which Gregg in her poem calls "grace" and Gibson, in hers, calls "words that let be." In the final three poems it is water: in Kenyon's, water that fills a stone trough, calming the anger of the person there; in Espada's, water of language so truthful it will put out the flames of repression; in Frost's, water we are asked to drink from a stream.

Robert Frost

Birches

When I see birches bend to left and right
Across the lines of straighter darker trees,
I like to think some boy's been swinging them.
But swinging doesn't bend them down to stay
As ice-storms do. Often you must have seen them
Loaded with ice a sunny winter morning
After a rain. They click upon themselves
As the breeze rises, and turn many-colored
As the stir cracks and crazes their enamel.
Soon the sun's warmth makes them shed crystal shells
Shattering and avalanching on the snow-crust—
Such heaps of broken glass to sweep away
You'd think the inner dome of heaven had fallen.
They are dragged to the withered bracken by the load,
And they seem not to break; though once they are bowed
So low for long, they never right themselves:
You may see their trunks arching in the woods
Years afterwards, trailing their leaves on the ground
Like girls on hands and knees that throw their hair
Before them over their heads to dry in the sun.
But I was going to say when Truth broke in
With all her matter-of-fact about the ice-storm
I should prefer to have some boy bend them
As he went out and in to fetch the cows—
Some boy too far from town to learn baseball,
Whose only play was what he found himself,
Summer or winter, and could play alone.
One by one he subdued his father's trees
By riding them down over and over again
Until he took the stiffness out of them,
And not one but hung limp, not one was left

For him to conquer. He learned all there was
To learn about not launching out too soon
And so not carrying the tree away
Clear to the ground. He always kept his poise
To the top branches, climbing carefully
With the same pains you use to fill a cup
Up to the brim, and even above the brim.
Then he flung outward, feet first, with a swish,
Kicking his way down through the air to the ground.
So was I once myself a swinger of birches.
And so I dream of going back to be.
It's when I'm weary of considerations,
And life is too much like a pathless wood
Where your face burns and tickles with the cobwebs
Broken across it, and one eye is weeping
From a twig's having lashed across it open.
I'd like to get away from earth awhile
And then come back to it and begin over.
May no fate willfully misunderstand me
And half grant what I wish and snatch me away
Not to return. Earth's the right place for love:
I don't know where it's likely to go better.
I'd like to go by climbing a birch tree,
And climb black branches up a snow-white trunk
Toward heaven, till the tree could bear no more,
But dipped its top and set me down again.
That would be good both going and coming back.
One could do worse than be a swinger of birches.

Wallace Stevens

Martial Cadenza

I

Only this evening I saw again low in the sky
The evening star, at the beginning of winter, the star
That in spring will crown every western horizon,
Again . . . as if it came back, as if life came back,
Not in a later son, a different daughter, another place,
But as if evening found us young, still young,
Still walking in a present of our own.

II

It was like sudden time in a world without time,
This world, this place, the street in which I was,
Without time: as that which is not has no time,
Is not, or is of what there was, is full
Of the silence before the armies, armies without
Either trumpets or drums, the commanders mute, the arms
On the ground, fixed fast in a profound defeat.

III

What had this star to do with the world it lit,
With the blank skies over England, over France
And above the German camps? It looked apart.
Yet it is this that shall maintain—Itself
Is time, apart from any past, apart
From any future, the ever-living and being,
The ever-breathing and moving, the constant fire,

IV

The present close, the present realized,
Not the symbol but that for which the symbol stands,
The vivid thing in the air that never changes,
Though the air change. Only this evening I saw it again,
At the beginning of winter, and I walked and talked
Again, and lived and was again, and breathed again
And moved again and flashed again, time flashed again.

Archibald MacLeish

Where the Hayfields Were

Coming down the mountain in the twilight—
April it was and quiet in the air—
I saw an old man and his little daughter
Burning the meadows where the hayfields were.

Forksful of flame he scattered in the meadows.
Sparkles of fire in the quiet air
Burned in their circles and the silver flowers
Danced like candles where the hayfields were,—

Danced as she did in enchanted circles,
Curtseyed and danced along the quiet air:
Slightly she danced in the stillness, in the twilight,
Dancing in the meadows where the hayfields were.

Robert Francis

The Sound I Listened For

What I remember is the ebb and flow of sound
That summer morning as the mower came and went
And came again, crescendo and diminuendo,
And always when the sound was loudest how it ceased
A moment while he backed the horses for the turn,
The rapid clatter giving place to the slow click
And the mower's voice. That was the sound I listened for.
The voice did what the horses did. It shared the action
As sympathetic magic does or incantation.
The voice hauled and the horses hauled. The strength of one
Was in the other and in the strength was no impatience.
Over and over as the mower made his rounds
I heard his voice and only once or twice he backed
And turned and went ahead and spoke no word at all.

Richard Eberhart

On a Squirrel Crossing the Road
in Autumn, in New England

It is what he does not know,
Crossing the road under the elm trees,
About the mechanism of my car,
About the Commonwealth of Massachusetts,
About Mozart, India, Arcturus,

That wins my praise. I engage
At once in whirling squirrel-praise.

He obeys the orders of nature
Without knowing them.
It is what he does not know
That makes him beautiful.
Such a knot of little purposeful nature!

I who can see him as he cannot see himself
Repose in the ignorance that is his blessing.

It is what man does not know of God
Composes the visible poem of the world.
                          . . . Just missed him!

Robert Penn Warren

Timeless, Twinned

Angelic, lonely, autochthonous, one white
Cloud lolls, unmoving, on an azure which
Is called the sky, and in gold drench of light,
No leaf, however gold, may stir, nor a single blade twitch,

Though autumn-honed, of the cattail by the pond. No voice
Speaks, since here no voice knows
The language in which a tongue might now rejoice.
So silence, a transparent flood, thus overflows.

In it, I drown, and from my depth my gaze
Yearns, faithful, toward that cloud's integrity,
As though I've now forgotten all other nights and days,
Anxiety born of the future's snare, or the nag of history.

What if, to my back, thin-shirted, brown grasses yet bring
The heat of summer, or beyond the perimeter northward, wind,
Snow-bellied, lurks? I stare at the cloud, white, motionless. I cling
To our single existence, timeless, twinned.

Stanley Kunitz

The Snakes of September

All summer I heard them
rustling in the shrubbery,
outracing me from tier
to tier in my garden,
a whisper among the viburnums,
a signal flashed from the hedgerow,
a shadow pulsing
in the barberry thicket.
Now that the nights are chill
and the annuals spent,
I should have thought them gone,
in a torpor of blood
slipped to the nether world
before the sickle frost.
Not so. In the deceptive balm
of noon, as if defiant of the curse
that spoiled another garden,
these two appear on show
through a narrow slit
in the dense green brocade
of a north-country spruce,
dangling head-down, entwined
in a brazen love-knot.
I put out my hand and stroke
the fine, dry grit of their skins.
After all,
we are partners in this land,
co-signers of a covenant.
At my touch the wild
braid of creation
trembles.

Constance Carrier

Journey

Between this and that other country
is neither barricade nor sentry.

Plausible under elm and maple
past the train window move the people,

no foreign air in face or clothing,
nothing to warn me, nothing, nothing—

no signboard's word to tell me whether
this is one country or the other.

Yet once arrived, without confusion
I move expertly thro the station:

no stranger whom the traffic vexes,
I can evade the trucks and taxis:

sure-footed sleepwalker, I saunter
across the park, see without wonder

the War Memorial, the benches,
familiar sun, familiar branches.

I wait the proper bus, and, waiting,
hear my name called in sudden greeting—

and find my own responses come
apt in the local idiom.

Elizabeth Bishop

Anaphora

In memory of Marjorie Carr Stevens

Each day with so much ceremony
begins, with birds, with bells,
with whistles from a factory;
such white-gold skies our eyes
first open on, such brilliant walls
that for a moment we wonder
"Where is the music coming from, the energy?
The day was meant for what ineffable creature
we must have missed?" Oh promptly he
appears and takes his earthly nature
    instantly, instantly falls
    victim of long intrigue,
    assuming memory and mortal
    mortal fatigue.

More slowly falling into sight
and showering into stippled faces,
darkening, condensing all his light;
in spite of all the dreaming
squandered upon him with that look,
suffers our uses and abuses,
sinks through the drift of bodies,
sinks through the drift of classes
to evening to the beggar in the park
who, weary, without lamp or book
    prepares stupendous studies:
    the fiery event
    of every day in endless
    endless assent.

Robert Lowell

Hawthorne

Follow its lazy main street lounging
from the alms house to Gallows Hill
along a flat, unvaried surface
covered with wooden houses
aged by yellow drain
like the unhealthy hair of an old dog.
You'll walk to no purpose
in Hawthorne's Salem.

I cannot resilver the smudged plate.

I drop to Hawthorne, the customs officer,
measuring coal and mostly trying to keep warm—
to the stunted black schooner,
the dismal South-end dock,
the wharf-piles with their fungus of ice.
On State Street
a steeple with a glowing dial-clock
measures the weary hours,
the merciless march of professional feet.

Even this shy distrustful ego
sometimes walked on top of the blazing roof,
and felt those flashes
that char the discharged cells of the brain.

Look at the faces—
Longfellow, Lowell, Holmes and Whittier!
Study the grizzled silver of their beards.
Hawthorne's picture,
however, has a blond mustache

and golden General Custer scalp.
He looks like a Civil War officer.
He shines in the firelight. His hard
survivor's smile is touched with fire.

Leave him alone for a moment or two,
and you'll see him with his head
bent down, brooding, brooding,
eyes fixed on some chip,
some stone, some common plant,
the commonest thing,
as if it were the clue.
The disturbed eyes rise,
furtive, foiled, dissatisfied
from meditation on the true
and insignificant.

William Meredith

The Cheer

reader my friend, is in the words here, somewhere.
Frankly, I'd like to make you smile.
Words addressing evil won't turn evil back
but they can give heart.
The cheer is hidden in right words.

A great deal isn't right, as they say,
as they are lately at some pains to tell us.
Words have to speak about that.
They would be the less words
for saying *smile* when they should say *do*.
If you ask them *do what?*
they turn serious quick enough, but never unlovely.
And they will tell you what to do,
if you listen, if you want that.

Certainly good cheer has never been what's wrong,
though solemn people mistrust it.
Against evil, between evils, lovely words are right.
How absurd it would be to spin these noises out,
so serious that we call them poems,
if they couldn't make a person smile.
Cheer or courage is what they were all born in.
It's what they're trying to tell us, miming like that.
It's native to the words,
and what they want us always to know,
even when it seems quite impossible to do.

Hayden Carruth

Song: So Often, So Long I Have Thought
for Cynthia Tokumitsu

So often, so long I have thought of death
That the fear has softened. It has worn away.
Strange. Here in autumn again, late October,
I am late too, my woodshed still half empty,
And hurriedly I split these blocks in the rain,
Maple and beech. South three hundred miles
My mother lies sterile and white in the room
Of her great age, her pain, while I myself
Have come to the edge of the "vale." Strange.
Hurrying to our ends, the generations almost
Collide, pushing one another. And in twilight
The October raindrops thicken and turn to snow.

Cindy stacks while I split, here where I once
Worked alone, my helper now younger than I
By more years than I am younger than my mother—
Cindy, fresh as the snow petals forming on this old
Goldenrod. Before her, it was war-time. In my work
I wondered about those unarmed Orientals swarming
Uphill into the machine guns, or those earlier
Who had gone smiling to be roasted in the bronze
Cauldrons, or the Cappadocian children strewn—
Strewn, strewn, and my horror uncomprehending. Were they
People, killers and killed, real people? In twilight
The October raindrops thickened and turned to snow.

I understand now. Not thoughtfully, never;
But I feel an old strange personal unconcern,
How my mother, I, even Cindy might vanish
And still the twilight fall. Something has made me
A man of the soil at last, like those old
Death-takers. And has consciousness, once so dear,
Worn down like theirs, to run in the dim
Seasonal continuance? Year by year my hands
Grow to the axe. Is there a comfort now
In this? Or shall I still, and ultimately, rebel,
As I had resolved to do? I look at Cindy in the twilight.
In her hair the thick October raindrops turn to snow.

Richard Wilbur

Advice to a Prophet

When you come, as you soon must, to the streets of our city,
Mad-eyed from stating the obvious,
Not proclaiming our fall but begging us
In God's name to have self-pity,

Spare us all word of the weapons, their force and range,
The long numbers that rocket the mind;
Our slow, unreckoning hearts will be left behind,
Unable to fear what is too strange.

Nor shall you scare us with talk of the death of the race.
How should we dream of this place without us?—
The sun mere fire, the leaves untroubled about us,
A stone look on the stone's face?

Speak of the world's own change. Though we cannot conceive
Of an undreamt thing, we know to our cost
How the dreamt cloud crumbles, the vines are blackened by frost,
How the view alters. We could believe,

If you told us so, that the white-tailed deer will slip
Into perfect shade, grown perfectly shy,
The lark avoid the reaches of our eye,
The jack-pine lose its knuckled grip

On the cold ledge, and every torrent burn
As Xanthus once, its gliding trout
Stunned in a twinkling. What should we be without
The dolphin's arc, the dove's return,

These things in which we have seen ourselves and spoken?
Ask us, prophet, how we shall call
Our natures forth when that live tongue is all
Dispelled, that glass obscured or broken

In which we have said the rose of our love and the clean
Horse of our courage, in which beheld
The singing locust of the soul unshelled,
And all we mean or wish to mean.

Ask us, ask us whether with the worldless rose
Our hearts shall fail us; come demanding
Whether there shall be lofty or long standing
When the bronze annals of the oak-tree close.

Alan Dugan

Thesis, Antithesis, and Nostalgia

Not even dried-up leaves,
skidding like iceboats on
their points down winter streets,
can scratch the surface of
a child's summer and its wealth:
a stagnant calm that seemed
as if it must go on and on
outside of cyclical variety
the way, at child-height on a wall,
a brick named "Ann"
by someone's piece of chalk
still loves the one named "Al"
although the street is vacant and
the writer and the named are gone.

Maxine Kumin

The Excrement Poem

It is done by us all, as God disposes, from
the least cast of worm to what must have been
in the case of the brontosaur, say, spoor
of considerable heft, something awesome.

We eat, we evacuate, survivors that we are.
I think these things each morning with shovel
and rake, drawing the risen brown buns
toward me, fresh from the horse oven, as it were,

or culling the alfalfa-green ones, expelled
in a state of ooze, through the sawdust bed
to take a serviceable form, as putty does,
so as to lift out entire from the stall.

And wheeling to it, storming up the slope,
I think of the angle of repose the manure
pile assumes, how sparrows come to pick
the redelivered grain, how inky-cap

coprinus mushrooms spring up in a downpour.
I think of what drops from us and must then
be moved to make way for the next and next.
However much we stain the world, spatter

it with our leavings, make stenches, defile
the great formal oceans with what leaks down,
trundling off today's last barrowful,
I honor shit for saying: We go on.

Philip Booth

Presence
    after George Oppen

That we are here: that we can question who
we are, where; that we relate to how deer

once small have grown bold in our back garden;
that we can ask, ask even ourselves, how

to the other we may appear, here in the always near place
we seem to ourselves to inhabit, who sleep toward

and wake from steeped hills, the sea opening into our eyes
the infinite possibility of infinity

we believe we're neither beyond nor shy of,
here as we are, without doubt, amid then, there,

and now, falling through dark into light, and back,
against which we cannot defend, wish as we might, as we do.

Still, as the physicist said, *the mystery is*
that we are here, here at all, still bearing with,

and borne by, all we try to make sense of:
this evening two does and a fawn who browse

the head lettuce we once thought was ours.
But no. As we chase them off mildly, and make

an odd salad of what they left us, the old stars
come casually out, and we see near and far we own nothing:

it's us who belong to all else; who, given this day,
are touched by, and touch, our tenderest knowing,

our lives incalculably dear as we feel for each other,
our skin no more or less thin than that of redwing,

rainbow, star-nose, or whitethroat, enfolded like us
in the valleys and waves of this irrefutable planet.

Galway Kinnell

Saint Francis and the Sow

The bud
stands for all things,
even for those things that don't flower,
for everything flowers, from within, of self-blessing;
though sometimes it is necessary
to reteach a thing its loveliness,
to put a hand on its brow
of the flower
and retell it in words and in touch
it is lovely
until it flowers again from within, of self-blessing;
as Saint Francis
put his hand on the creased forehead
of the sow, and told her in words and in touch
blessings of earth on the sow, and the sow
began remembering all down her thick length,
from the earthen snout all the way
through the fodder and slops to the spiritual curl of the tail,
from the hard spininess spiked out from the spine
down through the great broken heart
to the sheer blue milken dreaminess spurting and shuddering
from the fourteen teats into the fourteen mouths sucking and
     blowing beneath them:
the long, perfect loveliness of sow.

Anne Sexton

I Remember

By the first of August
the invisible beetles began
to snore and the grass was
as tough as hemp and was
no color—no more than
the sand was a color and
we had worn our bare feet
bare since the twentieth
of June and there were times
we forgot to wind up your
alarm clock and some nights
we took our gin warm and neat
from old jelly glasses while
the sun blew out of sight
like a red picture hat and
one day I tied my hair back
with a ribbon and you said
that I looked almost like
a puritan lady and what
I remember best is that
the door to your room was
the door to mine.

Donald Hall

Granite and Grass

1

On Ragged Mountain birches twist from rifts in granite.
Great ledges show gray through sugarbush. Brown bears
doze all winter under granite outcroppings or in cellarholes
the first settlers walled with fieldstone.
Granite markers recline in high abandoned graveyards.

Although split by frost or dynamite, granite is unaltered;
earthquakes tumble boulders across meadows; glaciers
carry pebbles with them as they grind south
and melt north, scooping lakes for the Penacook's trout.
Stone bulks, reflects sunlight, bears snow, and persists.

When highway-makers cut through a granite hill, scoring
deep trench-sides with vertical drillings, they leave behind
glittering sculptures, monuments to the granite state
of nature, emblems of permanence
that we worship in daily disease, and discover in stone.

2

But when we climb Ragged Mountain past cordwood stumpage,
over rocks of a dry creekbed, in company of young hemlock,
only granite remains unkind. Uprising in summer, in woods
and high pastures, our sister the fern breathes, trembles,
and alters, delicate fronds outspread and separate.

The fox pausing for scent cuts holes in hoarfrost.
Quail scream in the fisher's jaw; then the fisher dotes.
The coy-dog howls, raising puppies that breed more puppies
to rip the throats of rickety deer in March.
The moose's antlers extend, defending his wife for a season.

Mother-and-father grass lifts in the forsaken meadow,
grows tall under sun and rain, uncut, turns yellow,
sheds seeds, and under assault of snow relents; in May
green generates again. When the bear dies, bees construct
honey from nectar of cinquefoil growing through rib bones.

3

Ragged Mountain was granite before Adam divided.
Grass lives because it dies. If weary of discord
we gaze heavenward through the same eye that looks at us,
vision makes light of contradiction:
Granite is grass in the holy meadow of the soul's repose.

John Hollander

One of Our Walks

We ramble along up-hill through the woods, following
No path but knowing our direction generally,
And letting fall what may we come up against the worn
Fact that all this green is second growth—reaches of wall
Knee-high keep appearing among low moments of leaf;
Clearings, lit aslant, are strewn across old foundations.
This is of course New England now and even the brook,
Whose amplified whisper off on the right is as firm
A guide as any assured blue line on a roadmap,
Can never run clear of certain stones, those older forms
Of ascription of meaning to its murmuring, as
We hear it hum *O, I may come and I may go, but* . . .
Half-ruined in the white noise of its splashing water.

Derek Walcott

The Season of Phantasmal Peace

Then all the nations of birds lifted together
the huge net of the shadows of this earth
in multitudinous dialects, twittering tongues,
stitching and crossing it. They lifted up
the shadows of long pines down trackless slopes,
the shadows of glass-faced towers down evening streets,
the shadow of a frail plant on a city sill—
the net rising soundless as night, the birds' cries soundless, until
there was no longer dusk, or season, decline, or weather,
only this passage of phantasmal light
that not the narrowest shadow dared to sever.

And men could not see, looking up, what the wild geese drew,
what the ospreys trailed behind them in silvery ropes
that flashed in the icy sunlight; they could not hear
battalions of starlings waging peaceful cries,
bearing the net higher, covering this world
like the vines of an orchard, or a mother drawing
the trembling gauze over the trembling eyes
of a child fluttering to sleep;
                                        it was the light
that you will see at evening on the side of a hill
in yellow October, and no one hearing knew
what change had brought into the raven's cawing,
the killdeer's screech, the ember-circling chough

such an immense, soundless, and high concern
for the fields and cities where the birds belong,
except it was their seasonal passing, Love,
made seasonless, or, from the high privilege of their birth,
something brighter than pity for the wingless ones
below them who shared dark holes in windows and in houses,
and higher they lifted the net with soundless voices
above all change, betrayals of falling suns,
and this season lasted one moment, like the pause
between dusk and darkness, between fury and peace,
but, for such as our earth is now, it lasted long.

Sylvia Plath

Poems, Potatoes

The word, defining, muzzles; the drawn line
Ousts mistier peers and thrives, murderous,
In establishments which imagined lines

Can only haunt. Sturdy as potatoes,
Stones, without conscience, word and line endure,
Given an inch. Not that they're gross (although

Afterthought often would have them alter
To delicacy, to poise) but that they
Shortchange me continuously: whether

More or other, they still dissatisfy.
Unpoemed, unpictured, the potato
Bunches its knobby browns on a vastly
Superior page; the blunt stone also.

Brendan Galvin

Great Blue

Often,
around certain backwaters
like the ponds behind the oyster shacks,
I hope for a heron,

and sometimes I'm granted
that wood-silver,
crooked-stick, channel-marker effect
of the loosened neck,

and that silence, humped like
an overburden of experience,
the weight it hauls in flight
from river to pond above a highway

when I look up at the mere
abstract silhouette *bird* but am taken
by the dragged beat of wings

translucent at their tips,
and the cocked spurs trawled behind,
and have to swerve to hold the lane.

But I never expected it this morning,
Mother, on the wall of this room
you share with strangers:

the Egyptian sign for the generation
of life, its wisp of feather
hairlike off the nape, among the old
in their own humped solitudes.

Reason, that chain-store item,
can deny this forever, but that bird
shadows us, at key moments is there,

its gumped-up look guarding justice,
longevity, the journey
of the good and diligent soul.

Charles Simic

Spring

This is what I saw—old snow on the ground,
Three blackbirds preening themselves,
And my neighbor stepping out in her nightdress
To hang her husband's shirts on the line.

The morning wind made them hard to pin.
It swept the dress so high above her knees,
She had to stop what she was doing
And have a good laugh, while covering herself.

Michael S. Harper

History as Apple Tree

Cocumscussoc is my village,
the western arm of Narragansett
Bay, Canonicus chief sachem;
black men escape into his tribe.

How does patent not breed heresy?
Williams came to my chief
for his tract of land,
hunted by mad Puritans,
founded Providence Plantation;
Seekonk where he lost
first harvest, building, plant,
then the bay from these natives:
he set up trade.
With Winthrop he bought
an island, *Prudence;*
two other, *Hope* and *Patience*
he named, though small.
His trading post at the cove;
Smith's at another close by.
We walk the Pequot trail
as artery or spring.

Wampanoags, Cowesets,
Nipmucks, Niantics,
came by canoe for the games;
matted bats, a goal line,
a deerskin filled with moss:
lacrosse. They danced;
we are told they gambled their souls.

In your apple orchard
legend conjures Williams' name;
he was an apple tree.
Buried on his own lot
off Benefit Street
a giant apple tree grew;
two hundred years later,
when the grave was opened,
dust and root grew
in his human skeleton:
bones became apple tree.

As black man I steal away
in the night to the apple tree,
place my arm in the rich grave,
black sachem on a family plot,
take up a chunk of apple root,
let it become my skeleton,
become my own myth:
my arm the historical branch,
my name the bruised fruit,
black human photograph: apple tree.

Wesley McNair

Hunt Walking

If you could be there
with the rest, coming out

of Vernondale's store
carrying bags

in late spring, and if,
looking far down the road

where the white houses waver
in heat, you could see

for the first time
since winter, old Hunt,

the crippled man, walking
by not quite falling

down first on one side,
then on the other

holding aloft the bony
wing of his cane,

you would understand why
they have stopped

on the porch by the sign
that says Yes We Are Open,

without knowing
where they are

going, or what it is
they hold in their hands.

Linda Gregg

Esta

I think of him overturning the tables of the money
changers and the stalls of the sellers of doves.
I think of the outside of my house where most days
there are morning glories and sun on the gentians.
I go to the river by the dirt road between cornfields
under open skies to the shade and ferns and freshness
by the water. The current is powerful against me
as I swim upstream. I reach a tree that has fallen
into the river and hold on, breathing and excited
by the bright world. When I swim back to the shallows,
there are five Puerto Rican men fishing, two adults
and three boys. *Hola,* I say. One of the boys
says he is learning English. *El rio es frio,* I say.
The older man says *esta,* correcting me. When I get
out and start for my towel no one looks at me.
As I leave, the boy says quietly to his father,
Eso linda. I hold on to that grace as I ride
my bicycle back through the corn, the sun on me.

Louise Gluck

The Red Poppy

The great thing
is not having
a mind. Feelings:
oh, I have those; they
govern me. I have
a lord in heaven
called the sun, and open
for him, showing him
the fire of my own heart, fire
like his presence.
What could such glory be
if not a heart? Oh my brothers and sisters,
were you like me once, long ago,
before you were human? Did you
permit yourselves
to open once, who would never
open again? Because in truth
I am speaking now
the way you do. I speak
because I am shattered.

Margaret Gibson

Learning a New Language

When I tell you I've waked as if in a basement,
and the windows are open, I can smell roots—
don't do anything, you say, *just stand there.*

And simply, I am waiting.
Even learning Spanish in the evenings
I'm waiting, as if for a stump cut down
years back to send up one sapling
wet with new leaves.

Or sometimes, looking around the room I find you
here on the sofa, head tipped back to music,
learning what it means to open.
Then each new word gives me
your upturned face:
la cara, the face; *la ceja*
eyebrow; *la nariz,* the nose;
temple, *la sien; la boca*
the mouth.

And I remember the darkness, how the sea climbs
out of it, and the firmament, and light—
tentative at first, a dawn full of wind
and words that let be.

Jane Kenyon

Portrait of a Figure near Water

Rebuked, she turned and ran
uphill to the barn. Anger, the inner
arsonist, held a match to her brain.
She observed her life: against her will
it survived the unwavering flame.

The barn was empty of animals.
Only a swallow tilted
near the beams, and bats
hung from the rafters
the roof sagged between.

Her breath became steady
where, years past, the farmer cooled
the big tin amphorae of milk.
The stone trough was still
filled with water: she watched it
and received its calm.

So it is when we retreat in anger:
we think we burn alone
and there is no balm.
Then water enters, though it makes
no sound.

Martín Espada

When Songs Become Water

for Diario Latino,
El Salvador, 1991

Where dubbed commercials
sell the tobacco and alcohol
of a far winter metropolis,
where the lungs of night
cough artillery shots
into the ears of sleep,
where strikers with howls
stiff on their faces
and warnings pinned to their shirts
are harvested from garbage heaps,
where olive uniforms keep watch
over the plaza
from a nest of rifle eyes and sandbags,
where the government party
campaigns chanting through loudspeakers
that this country
will be the common grave of the reds,
there the newsprint of mutiny
is as medicine
on the fingertips,
and the beat of the press printing mutiny
is like the pounding of tortillas in the hands.

When the beat of the press
is like the pounding of tortillas,
and the newsprint is medicine
on the fingertips,
come the men with faces
wiped away by the hood,
who smother the mouth of witness night,
shaking the gasoline can across the floor,
then scattering in a dark orange eruption
of windows,
leaving the paper to wrinkle gray in the heat.

Where the faces wiped away by the hood
are known by the breath of gasoline
on their clothes,
and paper wrinkles gray as the skin
of incarcerated talkers,
another Army helicopter plunges from the sky
with blades burning
like the wings of a gargoyle,
the tortilla and medicine words
are smuggled in shawls,
the newspapers are hoarded
like bundles of letters from the missing,
the poems become songs
and the songs become water
streaming throught the arteries
of the earth, where others at the well
will cool the sweat in their hair
and begin to think.

Robert Frost

Directive

Back out of all this now too much for us,
Back in a time made simple by the loss
Of detail, burned, dissolved, and broken off
Like graveyard marble sculpture in the weather,
There is a house that is no more a house
Upon a farm that is no more a farm
And in a town that is no more a town.
The road there, if you'll let a guide direct you
Who only has at heart your getting lost,
May seem as if it should have been a quarry—
Great monolithic knees the former town
Long since gave up pretense of keeping covered.
And there's a story in a book about it:
Besides the wear of iron wagon wheels
The ledges show lines ruled southeast northwest,
The chisel work of an enormous Glacier
That braced his feet against the Arctic Pole.
You must not mind a certain coolness from him
Still said to haunt this side of Panther Mountain.
Nor need you mind the serial ordeal
Of being watched from forty cellar holes
As if by eye pairs out of forty firkins.
As for the woods' excitement over you
That sends light rustle rushes to their leaves,
Charge that to upstart inexperience.
Where were they all not twenty years ago?
They think too much of having shaded out
A few old pecker-fretted apple trees.
Make yourself up a cheering song of how
Someone's road home from work this once was,

Who may be just ahead of you on foot
Or creaking with a buggy load of grain.
The height of the adventure is the height
Of country where two village cultures faded
Into each other. Both of them are lost.
And if you're lost enough to find yourself
By now, pull in your ladder road behind you
And put a sign up CLOSED to all but me.
Then make yourself at home. The only field
Now left's no bigger than a harness gall.
First there's the children's house of make believe,
Some shattered dishes underneath a pine,
The playthings in the playhouse of the children.
Weep for what little things could make them glad.
Then for the house that is no more a house,
But only a belilaced cellar hole,
Now slowly closing like a dent in dough.
This was no playhouse but a house in earnest.
Your destination and your destiny's
A brook that was the water of the house,
Cold as a spring as yet so near its source,
Too lofty and original to rage.
(We know the valley streams that when aroused
Will leave their tatters hung on barb and thorn.)
I have kept hidden in the instep arch
Of an old cedar at the waterside
A broken drinking goblet like the Grail
Under a spell so the wrong ones can't find it,
So can't get saved, as Saint Mark says they mustn't.
(I stole the goblet from the children's playhouse.)
Here are your waters and your watering place.
Drink and be whole again beyond confusion.

Brief Biographies

Born in Reading, Pennsylvania, **Wallace Stevens** (1879–1955) was educated at Harvard and the New York Law School. In 1916 he joined the Hartford Accident and Indemnity Company, serving as vice president from 1934 until his decease. He published his first book of poems in 1923. His fifth, *The Auroras of Autumn* (1950), received the Pulitzer Prize and the National Book Award, both given once again for his *Collected Poems* (Knopf, 1954).

Born in Glencoe, Illinois, **Archibald MacLeish** (1892–1982) graduated from Yale and Harvard Law School and served as a field artillery officer in WWI. He gave up law to write, in France, then here, publishing prose, drama, and the poetic work included in *New and Collected Poems* (Houghton Mifflin, 1985). Recipient of three Pulitzer prizes, he was Assistant Secretary of State and Librarian of Congress. He lived in Conway, Massachusetts.

Born in Upland, Pennsylvania, **Robert Francis** (1901–1987) lived in Amherst, Massachusetts. Educated at Harvard, he taught briefly in high schools, then managed on the small income from his writing. Recipient of the Academy of American Poets Fellowship and other awards, he published, besides prose, the seven books reprinted in his *Collected Poems* (University of Massachusetts Press, 1976). His more recent work appears in *Late Fire, Late Snow*, published in 1992.

Richard Eberhart, born in Austin, Minnesota, in 1904, graduated from Dartmouth and Cambridge and was a Naval gunnery officer during WWII. He worked as assistant manager of the Butcher Polish Company and later taught at Dartmouth. Recipient of two Pulitzer prizes and the Bollingen Prize, he was 1978 Poet Laureate of New Hampshire. His poetry is available in *Collected Poems* (Oxford University Press, 1976) and *The Long Reach* (New Directions, 1983).

Born in Guthrie, Kentucky, **Robert Penn Warren** (1905–1989) was educated at Vanderbilt University, Yale, and Oxford and taught at Yale and other universities. He founded *The Southern Review* and was co-author of *Understanding Poetry*. Recipient of three Pulitzer prizes and other major awards, he published fiction, essays, and fourteen books of poetry, including *New and Selected Poems* (Random House, 1985) He lived in Connecticut and Vermont.

Born in Worcester, Massachusetts, in 1905, **Stanley Kunitz** was educated at Harvard, served in the U.S. Army in WWII, and taught at Columbia, Yale, and Princeton. He received the Pulitzer and Bollingen prizes and was Poetry Consultant to the Library of Congress. His books include *The Poems of Stanley Kunitz* (Little, Brown, 1979), *Next to Last Things* (Atlantic Monthly Press, 1985), and *Passing Through* (Norton, 1995). Kunitz is a resident of Provincetown, Massachusetts.

Constance Carrier (1908–1991), born in New Britain, Connecticut, graduated from Smith, took an M.A. at Trinity, and taught Latin in New Britain and West Hartford schools. Her first book, *The Middle Voice*, received the Poetry Society of America Prize and was the Lamont Poetry Selection of 1954. Besides translations from Propertius and Tubullus, she published two other collections, lastly *Witchcraft Poems: Salem, 1692* (Stone House, 1988).

Born in Worcester, Massachusetts, **Elizabeth Bishop** (1911–1979) grew up in New England and Nova Scotia and was educated at Vassar. She lived in Key West and Brazil and in later years taught at Harvard. Recipient of the Pulitzer Prize, the National Book Critics Circle Award, and the Academy of American Poets Fellowship, she published eight volumes, all included in her *Complete Poems* (Farrar, Straus & Giroux, 1983). Her *Collected Prose* was published in 1984.

Robert Lowell (1917–1977) was born in Boston and attended Harvard, Kenyon College, and Louisiana State University. As a conscientious objector, he served a six-month jail sentence during WWII. Recipient of two Pulitzer prizes, the Bollingen Prize, the National Book Award, and the National Book Critics Circle Award, he taught at Yale, Oxford, and Harvard. Poetry from eight of his books is included in *Selected Poems* (Farrar, Straus & Giroux, 1976).

Born in New York in 1919, **William Meredith** graduated from Princeton, served as a naval aviator in the Pacific in WWII, and taught primarily at Connecticut College. He helped direct the Upward Bound program in the 1960's and was Poetry Consultant to the Library of Congress. His other honors include a National Endowment for the Arts senior fellowship and the Pulitzer Prize for his new and selected poems, *Partial Accounts* (Knopf, 1987).

Born in Waterbury, Connecticut, in 1921, **Hayden Carruth** was educated at the universities of North Carolina and Chicago and served in Italy in WWII. He edited *Poetry* magazine and taught at Syracuse University and the University of Vermont. Among his awards are the Ruth Lilly Poetry Prize, a National Endowment for the Arts senior fellowship, the Vermont Governor's Medal, and the 1995 Lannan Literary Award. Poems from nine of his books are included in his *Selected Poetry* (Macmillan, 1986).

Richard Wilbur, born in New York in 1921, was educated at Amherst and Harvard, served with the infantry in Italy during WWII, and taught at Wellesley, Wesleyan, and Smith. A Poet Laureate of the United States, he has received the National Book Award, the National Medal of the Arts, and two Pulitzer prizes, the second for his *New and Collected Poems* (Harcourt Brace, 1988). Besides lyric poetry, he has written highly acclaimed translations from Molière and Racine. Wilbur is a resident of Cummington, Massachusetts.

Born in Brooklyn, New York, in 1923, **Alan Dugan** lives in Truro, Massachusetts. He served in the U.S. Army Air Force in WWII, graduated from Mexico City College, and worked in advertising and as a model maker for a medical supply house. *Poems* (1961) received the Yale Younger Poets Award, the National Book Award, and the Pulitzer Prize. His most recent book is *Poems 6* (Ecco Press, 1989). He teaches at the Fine Arts Work Center in Provincetown.

Born in Philadelphia in 1925, **Maxine Kumin** was educated at Radcliffe and has taught at Columbia, Princeton, and M.I.T. She has served as Poetry

Consultant to the Library of Congress, and her other honors include the Academy of American Poets fellowship and the 1973 Pulitzer Prize for *Up Country*. She has published fiction, essays, and eleven volumes of poetry, recently *Connecting the Dots* (Norton, 1996). She lives on a farm in Warner, New Hampshire.

Philip Booth, born in 1925 in Hanover, New Hampshire, was educated at Dartmouth and Columbia and lives in Castine, Maine. He has taught at Bowdoin, Dartmouth, Wellesley, and Syracuse University. His honors include the Lamont Poetry Selection and a National Endowment fellowship. He has published nine books of poetry, most recently *Pairs* (Penguin, 1994), and a collection of essays, *Trying to Say It* (University of Michigan Press, 1996).

Born in 1927 in Providence, Rhode Island, **Galway Kinnell** was educated at Princeton and the University of Rochester. A Vermont State Poet, he lives in Vermont and Manhattan and teaches at New York University. Besides fiction, criticism, and translations from Villon and other French poets, he has published twelve books of poetry. His *Selected Poems* received the American Book Award, the National Book Award, and the Pulitzer Prize. His most recent collection is *Imperfect Thirst* (Houghton Mifflin, 1994).

Anne Sexton (1928–1974) was raised in Wellesley, Massachusetts, attended Garland Junior College, and lived most of her life in Weston. Her eight poetry collections, one of which received the Pulitzer Prize, are included with other work in her *Complete Poems* (Houghton Mifflin, 1981). She taught at Radcliffe, Colgate, and Boston University. Plagued for years by severe depressions, Sexton died by suicide at the age of forty-five.

Born in 1928, **Donald Hall** grew up in Hamden, Connecticut, and on his grandparents' farm in Wilmot, New Hampshire. Educated at Harvard and Oxford, he taught for many years at the University of Michigan, then settled at the farm to write full time. Recipient of the National Book Critics Circle Award for his book-length poem *The One Day*, he has published essays, memoirs, fiction, and twelve volumes of poetry, eight represented in *Old and New Poems*. His most recent collection is *The Old Life* (Houghton Mifflin, 1996).

John Hollander was born in New York in 1929. He obtained a B.A. and M.A. at Columbia and a doctoral degree from Indiana University. Recipient of the Yale Younger Poets Award, a National Institute of Arts and Letters grant, a Guggenheim fellowship, and the Levinson Prize, he has published, besides critical essays and children's literature, sixteen poetry collections, eleven represented in his *Selected Poetry* (Knopf, 1993). Hollander teaches at Yale.

Born in 1930 on the island of St. Lucia, **Derek Walcott** was educated at the University of the West Indies, Jamaica, and teaches at Boston University. Beginning as a painter (he illustrates his own book jackets), he later turned to writing poetry and drama. His plays are produced in New York and London. His eleven books include his *Collected Poems* and the epic poem *Omeros* (Farrar, Straus & Giroux, 1990). Walcott was awarded the 1992 Nobel Prize for Literature.

Sylvia Plath (1932–1963) grew up in the Boston area, graduated from Smith, and attended Cambridge University on a Fulbright Scholarship. In 1956 she married the English poet Ted Hughes. They lived in Massachusetts and, with their two children, in England, where Plath died by suicide at age thirty. Her novel, *The Bell Jar*, was published posthumously, as were her *Collected Poems* (Harper & Row, 1981), which received the Pulitzer Prize.

Born in 1938 in- Everett, Massachusetts, **Brendan Galvin** was educated at Boston College, Northeastern University, and the University of Massachusetts. He teaches at Central Connecticut State University and spends half of each year in Truro, Cape Cod. Recipient of Guggenheim and National Endowment fellowships, he has published ten books of poetry, five of them represented in *Great Blue: New and Selected Poems*. His most recent collection is *Sky and Island Light* (Louisiana State University Press, 1996).

Born in Belgrade, Yugoslavia, in 1938, **Charles Simic** emigrated to this country in 1954. He graduated from New York University and teaches at the University of New Hampshire. Besides translations and criticism, he has published many works of poetry, including *Selected Poems* (Braziller, 1990). Among his honors are a National Endowment fellowship, a MacArthur fellowship, and the Pulitzer Prize. His most recent collection is *A Wedding in Hell* (Harcourt Brace, 1994).

Michael S. Harper, born in 1938 in Brooklyn, New York, earned a B.A. and M.A. at Los Angeles State College and an M.F.A. at the University of Iowa. Recipient of awards from the Black Academy of Arts and Letters, the National Institute of Arts and Letters, and the American Academy, he has published ten books of poems, among them *Images of Kin: New and Selected Poems* and *Honorable Amendments* (University of Illinois Press, 1995). He teaches at Brown.

Born in 1941 in Newport, New Hampshire, **Wesley McNair** was educated at Keene State and Middlebury colleges and teaches at the University of Maine. He has held a Guggenheim fellowship, as well as two fellowships from the National Endowment, and written an Emmy-award-winning television series on Frost. The most recent of his four books of poetry is *My Brother Running* (Godine, 1993). A fifth collection, *Love Handles,* is forthcoming.

Born in Suffern, New York, in 1942, **Linda Gregg** grew up in Marin County, California, and lives in Northampton, Massachusetts. She obtained a B.A. and an M.A. at San Francisco State College and has taught at numerous colleges, universities, and writers conferences. Recipient of National Endowment and Guggenheim fellowships, the Whiting Writers Award, and the Pushcart Prize, Gregg has published four poetry collections, recently *Chosen by the Lion* (Graywolf, 1994).

Born in New York in 1943, **Louise Gluck** attended Columbia and Sarah Lawrence. She has taught at many colleges and universities and has been teaching at Williams College since 1984. Her honors include three National Endowment fellowships, the Melville Kane Award, and the National Book Critics Circle Award for Poetry. Gluck has published eight books of poems, among them *The Wild Iris* (Ecco, 1992). She lives in Plainfield, Vermont.

Margaret Gibson, born in Philadelphia in 1944, graduated from Hollins College and took an M.A. at University of Virginia. She teaches at University of Connecticut and has worked as a tenants organizer in New London's Hispanic community. One of her five books, *Long Walks in the Afternoon,* was the 1982 Lamont Poetry Selection; another, *The Vigil* (Louisiana State University Press, 1993), was a finalist for the National Book Award. She lives in Preston, Connecticut.

Born in Ann Arbor and educated at the University of Michigan, **Jane Kenyon** (1947–1995) published translations from the poems of Anna Akhmatova and four poetry collections, including *Constance* (Graywolf, 1993), honored by the 1994 PEN/Voelcker Award. A National Endowment fellow and New Hampshire Poet Laureate, she lived in Wilmot with her husband Donald Hall. *Otherwise,* her new and selected poems, was published by Graywolf in 1996.

Born in Brooklyn, New York, in 1957, **Martín Espada** studied history at the University of Wisconsin and law at Northeastern University. He worked for sixteen years as an attorney in a legal services program for low-income tenants in Chelsea, Massachusetts, and presently teaches in the English Department at the University of Massachusetts in Amherst. Recipient of a National Endowment fellowship, he has published five books of poetry, recently *Imagine the Angels of Bread* (Norton, 1996).

Henry Lyman (editor) was born in 1942, grew up in Bloomfield, Connecticut, and was educated at Yale and the University of Massachusetts. He has published translations from the work of the Estonian poet Aleksis Rannit, edited Robert Francis's posthumously published collection *Late Fire, Late Snow*, and for many years hosted "Poems to a Listener," a national radio program of readings and interviews with poets. He lives in Northampton, Massachusetts.

Sources

The following works served as sources for the writing of the introduction. For a meticulously detailed account of Frost's life, the Thompson biography is invaluable. Pritchard's literary biography, Francis's memoir, and the shorter memoir included in Hall's book offer more balanced assessments of Frost's complex personality. Many of Frost's statements on poetry can be found in Barry's selection of letters, lectures, and prose.

Lawrance Thompson, *Robert Frost: The Early Years, 1874–1915.* (Holt, Rinehart and Winston, 1966).

Lawrance Thompson, *Robert Frost: The Years of Triumph, 1915–1938.* (Holt, Rinehart and Winston, 1970).

Lawrance Thompson and R. H. Winnick, *Robert Frost: The Later Years, 1938–1963.* (Holt, Rinehart and Winston, 1976).

Lawrance Thompson and R. H. Winnick, *Robert Frost: A Biography.* (Holt, Rinehart and Winston, 1981). This is a one-volume condensation of the three volumes mentioned above.

Selected Letters of Robert Frost, ed. Lawrance Thompson. (Holt, Rinehart and Winston, 1964).

Elaine Barry, *Robert Frost on Writing*. (Rutgers University Press, 1973).

William H. Pritchard, *Frost: A Literary Life Reconsidered*. (University of Massachusetts Press, 1993).

Robert Francis, *Frost: A Time to Talk*. (University of Massachusetts Press, 1972).

Donald Hall, *Their Ancient Glittering Eyes: Remembering Poets and More Poets*. (Ticknor and Fields, 1992).

Ralph Waldo Emerson, *Collected Works,* Vol. 1. (The Belknap Press, 1971).

Ralph Waldo Emerson, *Essays*. (The Belknap Press, 1987).

Notes to Introduction

⌒

p. 2 "A poem . . . thought finds the words":
Frost to Louis Untermeyer, 1 Jan. 1916, *Selected Letters,* p. 199.

p. 5 ". . . there is a kind of success . . . for all sorts and kinds":
Frost to John T. Bartlett, 5 Nov. 1913, *Selected Letters,* p. 98.

". . . every man is so far a poet . . . celebration":
Emerson, "The Poet," *Essays,* p. 227.

"man is only half himself":
Emerson, "The Poet," *Essays,* p. 222.

p. 6 "paper currency":
Emerson, "Nature," *Works,* p. 20.

"Poetry . . . stands as a reminder . . . renew ourselves":
Frost, quoted by Thompson, *The Years of Triumph,* p. 431.

"Piquancy . . . farmer or backwoodsman":
Emerson, "Nature," *Works,* p. 20.

"the hard everyday word of the street":
Frost, lecture, Browne and Nichols School, 13 March 1918,
Barry, *Frost on Writing, p. 145.*

"The actor's gift . . . fasten it to the page":
Frost, letter to J. Freeman, 5 Nov. 1925 [?], Barry, p. 80.

p. 8 "breaking the sounds of sense . . . beat of the metre":
Frost to J. Bartlett, 4 July 1913, *Selected Letters,* p. 80.

"I am never more pleased . . . strained relation":
Frost to J. Cournos, 8 July 1914, *Selected Letters,* p. 128.

p.11 "fasten words again to visible things":
Emerson, "Nature, *Works,* p. 20.

p.12 "there is no fact in nature . . . sense of nature":
Emerson, "The Poet,"*Essays,* p. 228.

"reattaches things to nature and the Whole":
Emerson, "The Poet," *Essays,* p. 229.

p. 21 "threat":
Frost, letter to L. Chase, 11 July 1917, and letter to A. Bonner,
7 June 1937, Barry, pp. 73–76.

"save":
Frost refers to "being saved" by art, as well as "being threatened,"
in a letter to A. Bonner, 7 June 1937, Barry, p. 76.

"a momentary stay against confusion":
Frost, "The Figure a Poem Makes," essay written 1939 as the
preface for his collected poems.

p.22 *"we're in this together":*
Margaret Gibson, "Long Walks in the Afternoon,"
After Frost, p. 67.

"In our way of talking . . . beautiful to him as to you":
Emerson, "The Poet," *Essays,* p. 339.

Acknowledgments

—

Grateful acknowledgment is made to the following publishers, authors, or other parties for permission to reprint the poems:

Elizabeth Bishop: "Anaphora," "In the Waiting Room," "Sandpiper," and "Varick Street" from *The Complete Poems 1927–1979*. Copyright © 1979, 1983 by Alice Helen Methfessel. Reprinted by permission of Farrar, Straus & Giroux, Inc.

Philip Booth: "Species" and "Supposition with Qualification" from *Relations: New and Selected Poems*, copyright © 1986 by Philip Booth; "Game" and "Presence" from *Selves*, copyright © 1990 by Philip Booth. Used by permission of Viking Penguin, a division of Penguin Books USA Inc.

Constance Carrier: "The Prospect Before Us," "Perspective," "Pro Patria," and "Journey" reprinted by permission of the Estate of Constance V. Carrier.

Hayden Carruth: "Lost" from *Collected Shorter Poems 1946–1991*. Copyright © 1992 by Hayden Carruth. Reprinted by permission of Copper Canyon Press, PO Box 271, Port Townsend, WA 98368. "The Loon on Forrester's Pond," "The Mountain," and "Song: So Often, So Long I Have Thought" from *The Selected Poetry of Hayden Carruth*. Reprinted by permission of the author.

Linda Gregg: "To Be Here" and "*Esta*" copyright 1991 by Linda Gregg. Reprinted from *The Sacraments of Desire* with the permission of Graywolf Press, Saint Paul, Minnesota. "The Copperhead" and "The Shopping–Bag Lady" reprinted by permission of the author.

Donald Hall: "Names of Horses" from *Old and New Poems*, copyright © 1990 by Donald Hall; excerpts from *The One Day*, copyright © 1988 by Donald Hall. Reprinted by permission of Ticknor & Fields / Houghton Mifflin Co. All rights reserved. "Mr. Wakeville on Interstate 90" and "Granite and Grass" from *The Happy Man*, copyright © 1981, 1982, 1983, 1984, 1986 by Donald Hall. Reprinted by permission of Random House, Inc.

Michael S. Harper: "Makin' Jump Shots" from *Images of Kin: New and Selected Poems*, © 1977 by Michael S. Harper. Reprinted by permission of the author and the University of Illinois Press. "The Drive In," "The Families Album," and "History as Apple Tree" from *Song: I Want a Witness*, copyright © 1972 by Michael S. Harper. Reprinted by permission of the University of Pittsburgh Press.

John Hollander: "Grounds of Winter," "A Late Fourth," "One of Our Walks," and "The Angler's Story" from Selected Poetry. Copyright © 1993 by John Hollander. Reprinted by permission of Alfred A. Knopf, Inc.

Jane Kenyon: "August Rain, after Haying" and "Potato" copyright 1993 by Jane Kenyon, reprinted from *Constance* with the permission of Graywolf Press, Saint Paul, Minnesota. "Back from the City" and "Portrait of a Figure near Water" copyright 1986 by Jane Kenyon, reprinted from *The Boat of Quiet Hours* with the permission of Graywolf Press, Saint Paul, Minnesota.

Galway Kinnell: "Farm Picture" from *The Past*, copyright © 1985 by Galway Kinnell; "Saint Francis and the Sow" from *Mortal Acts, Mortal Words*, copyright © 1980 by Galway Kinnell. Reprinted by permission of Houghton Mifflin Co. All rights reserved. "The Room" and "The Tragedy of Bricks" from *When One Has Lived a Long Time Alone*, copyright © 1990 by Galway Kinnell. Reprinted by permission of Alfred A. Knopf, Inc.

Maxine Kumin: "Saga" from *Looking For Luck*, copyright © 1992 by Maxine Kumin. Reprinted by permission of W. W. Norton & Company, Inc. "My Father's Neckties" and "The Excrement Poem" from *Our Ground Time Here Will Be Brief*, copyright © 1957–1965,1970–1982 by Maxine Kumin;

copyright © 1962 by Anne Sexton, renewed 1990 by Linda G. Sexton. Reprinted by permission of Houghton Mifflin Co. All rights reserved.

Charles Simic: "Windy Evening" from *The Book of Gods and Devils*, copyright © 1990 by Charles Simic; "Spring" from *Hotel Insomnia*, copyright © 1992 by Charles Simic. Reprinted by permission of Harcourt Brace & Company. "Shirt" and "Grocery" from *Classic Ballroom Dances* © Copyright 1980 by Charles Simic. Reprinted by permission of George Braziller, Inc.

Wallace Stevens: "The Snow Man" copyright 1923 and renewed 1951 by Wallace Stevens; "Less and Less Human, O Savage Spirit" copyright 1947 by Wallace Stevens; "Idiom of the Hero" copyright 1942 by Wallace Stevens; "Martial Cadenza" copyright 1942 and renewed 1970 by Holly Stevens. From *Collected Poems*. Reprinted by permission of Alfred A. Knopf, Inc.

Derek Walcott: Sections XXX and XXXI from *Midsummer*, copyright © 1984 by Derek Walcott.; "For Adrian" from The Arkansas Testament, copyright © 1987 by Derek Walcott; "The Season of Phantasmal Peace" from *Collected Poems 1948–1984*, copyright © 1986 by Derek Walcott. Reprinted by permission of Farrar, Straus & Giroux, Inc.

Robert Penn Warren: "Better Than Counting Sheep," "Dream, Dump-Heap, and Civilization," "Timeless, Twinned," and "Sky" from *Being Here: Poetry 1977–1980*, copyright © 1978, 1979, 1980 by Robert Penn Warren. Reprinted by permission of Random House, Inc.

Richard Wilbur: "An Event" from *Things of This World*, copyright © 1956 and renewed 1984 by Richard Wilbur; "In Limbo" from *The Mind-Reader*, copyright © 1975 by Richard Wilbur; "A Finished Man," from *New and Collected Poems*, copyright © 1985 by Richard Wilbur, originally appeared in The New Yorker; "Advice to a Prophet" from *Advice to a Prophet and Other Poems*, copyright © 1959 and renewed 1987 by Richard Wilbur. Reprinted by permission of Harcourt Brace & Company.